HIS TO TAME

Bears of Grizzly Ridge

ELENA AITKEN

Also by Elena Aitken

Bears of Grizzly Ridge

His to Protect

His to Seduce

His to Claim

Hers to Take

His to Defend

His to Tame

His to Seek

Hers for the Season

Bears of Grizzly Ridge: Books 1-4

Bears of Grizzly Ridge: Books 5-8

Ever After

Choosing Happily Ever After

Needing Happily Ever After

Wanting Happily Ever After

Fighting Happily Ever After

We Wish You A Happily Ever After

Keeping Happily Ever After

Finding Happily Ever After

Seeking Happily Ever After

Cherishing Happily Ever After

Ever After: Volume One (Books 1-4)

Stand Alone Stories

All We Never Knew

Drawing Free

Sugar Crash

Composing Myself

Betty & Veronica

The Escape Collection

Vegas

Nothing Stays in Vegas

Return to Vegas

Timber Creek

When We Left

When We Were Us

When We Began

When We Fell

Castle Mountain Lodge

Unexpected Gifts

Hidden Gifts

Unexpected Endings - Short Story

Mistaken Gifts

Secret Gifts

Goodbye Gifts

Tempting Gifts

Holiday Gifts

Promised Gifts

Accidental Gifts

The Castle Mountain Lodge Collection: Books 1-3

The Castle Mountain Lodge Collection: Books 4-6

The Castle Mountain Lodge Collection: Books 7-9

The Castle Mountain Lodge Complete Collection

Halfway Series

Halfway to Nowhere

Halfway in Between

Halfway to Christmas

Reader Note

You might not know…this book (and the entire series) is a little different than my usual contemporary romances.

But sometimes you have to try something a little different, and that was the case for me when it came to writing 'the bears'.

I had so much fun with this series at a time in my life when that's what I needed—fun. So much fun in fact that I needed to revisit Grizzly Ridge with four more sexy stories!!

I hope you have as much fun reading these new stories!

Chapter One

GRIZZLY RIDGE WAS the most beautiful place Zoe Karrington had been to in years. She could happily spend most of her day walking through the forest or sitting by the edge of the creek with her feet dangling in the cold water. She could do that, too, and more—if it weren't for her big sister Chloe harassing her every second. She'd finally been able to get a few moments of peace by sneaking away from the main lodge they called the Den—*how cute for an eco-lodge run by grizzly bear shifters*—and into the woods.

It wouldn't be long before Chloe tracked her down and dragged her back to the lodge, demanding some sort of answers about what she was doing with her life, why she was there, and where she'd been. All questions that Zoe did not feel like answering.

Mostly because she didn't have any answers that could possibly satisfy Chloe, who'd never done anything wrong in her entire life. And, of course, because Chloe would probably turn around and call their parents. Not that it mattered, not really. After all, Zoe was a grown woman. She could do what she wanted.

As long as what she was doing didn't ruffle any feathers.

She couldn't help but laugh at herself and her messed-up life. After all, if you couldn't laugh at yourself, who *could* you laugh at?

Zoe gave herself a few more minutes with her bare feet dangling in the cold water, pulling them out right before they went numb. It was already October, which meant that even if the sun was still shining, fall had definitely arrived. She tugged her socks and boots on and jumped to her feet. It was the perfect place to go for a run. To let her bear out and stretch her muscles. As much as she didn't want to admit it, especially to Chloe, from the little she'd seen so far, Grizzly Ridge was the perfect place for bear shifters.

Even for a black bear like herself, it might be a good place to settle down and make a life.

If making a life was what she wanted.

"Zoe!"

Right on cue.

There was no point running—again; her big sister would just find her. Especially considering Zoe had left her motorbike there. And there was no way she was running away from her brand-new Indian Chief Dark Horse motorbike. Not when she'd worked so hard to save up the money to have it custom built, with the sexy matte black paint job. It was everything. At least, it was everything she owned in the world.

If it meant having a sit-down with Chloe, she'd do it. Besides, she was the one who arrived unannounced at Grizzly Ridge. Maybe she, at the very least, owed Chloe some sort of explanation.

She pulled her long thick hair back to the crown of her head before letting it fall around her shoulders and took a moment to squeeze her eyes shut and take a deep breath before she turned to face her big sister, who had joined her at the bank of the stream.

"Hi, Chloe." Her voice dripped with syrupy sweetness, but Chloe only rolled her eyes.

"Where have you been?"

She was taller than her sister, but not by much, and although they were actually very similar in physical stature, Zoe tended to take up a lot more space than her older sister. She always had. As the youngest girl in their family—with two older sisters who got a lot of their parents' attention—Zoe had learned at an early age that if she wanted anyone to pay attention to her, she better stand out.

So she did.

When she was younger, that attention seeking had taken the form of being her parents' favorite. She was always seeking ways to please them and make them smile or laugh. She frequently put on small performances where she'd sing or play the piano or occasionally act out a play she'd written. In high school, she'd taken her talents to a larger stage and had shone in the spotlight. Zoe had thrived with the attention, but she'd always used her attention for good. She'd been popular and got good grades. She spent her days dreaming of the day she'd fall in love, find her mate, and settle down to raise a house full of babies.

Unlike most of her friends, or her big sister, Zoe had always looked forward to settling down. It had been her lifelong dream.

Until lately.

IT HAD BEEN a slow shift for Officer Gabe Wilder. Just the way he liked them. A lot of police officers thrived on the adrenaline of their shifts, craving some type of crime to take place so they could jump into action. Gabe liked it quiet. He was no stranger to conflict, and had no problem chasing down a perp, breaking up a domestic dispute, taking a drunk and disorderly into custody, or drawing his weapon if the situation called for it. But all that meant was that there was trouble in the valley—his home—and that was the last thing he wanted.

The quiet Montana mountain valley had become his home just a few years ago and despite the fact that his clan was from the West Coast, the local grizzly shifter community had embraced him as one of their own. It had taken awhile, but he was finally starting to feel at home there, and he didn't want anything to mess that up. Which was why he'd sworn to serve and protect the small town of Boulder Creek and the larger area of Jackson Valley, and of course Grizzly Ridge where a lot of his friends lived and ran the area's most popular, new eco-lodge travel destination.

But the area was growing, not in small part because of Grizzly Ridge. Their quiet valley was starting to become a more popular tourist destination, and with an increased population came an increase in crime. The days of Gabe's slow shifts were becoming fewer and further between. Especially considering there were only a handful of officers in the area. No doubt that would be another change.

Gabe ran his hand over his face and shook his head.

Change was inevitable.

But it didn't mean he had to like it.

Just then, a call came over the radio that reminded him exactly how much his small town was changing.

"Officer Wilder? Reports of a domestic disturbance on Fourth."

"I'm on it." Gabe spoke into the radio as he flipped the lights on the top of his cruiser. No point messing with a siren; he was only a few blocks away and given the address, he knew exactly what was going on.

Sure enough, as Gabe pulled up to the blue and white bungalow with the paint chipping off the porch, and more than one shutter either falling from its hinges or already on the ground, the scene on the front lawn was exactly what he expected.

Ashley Morris, a young single mom of three, who had a reputation of making all the wrong decisions when it came to her love life, stood on her front lawn, a baseball bat overhead. A man Gabe only vaguely recognized as one of the ranch hands from Blackwood Ranch up the road was on his back, using his elbows and feet fairly unsuccessfully to scoot down the lawn away from what looked like a very pissed-off Ashley.

"Whoa." Gabe got out of the car and walked over to the woman. He held his hands in front of him to show he came in peace. Ashley already knew he wasn't a threat. Gabe had done nothing but help her out when it came to getting rid of men who overstayed their welcome, or for whatever reason got the wrong idea about what it was she was looking for. Which was definitely not a deadbeat boyfriend hanging around causing more trouble than he was worth.

"Ashley." He took another step. "Give me the bat."

"I want him gone, Gabe."

"Officer, she's bat-shit crazy." The man on the ground, who clearly didn't have a full understanding of how dangerous a woman with a bat could be, piped up. "All I said was—"

"That she was your *sister*." Ashley raised the bat higher. "From what I saw, she is definitely not your sister!"

"She *is* my sister. Ash, I love you. You need to calm down."

"Don't tell me what to do!"

"Okay, okay." Gabe had to resist the urge to laugh. It wasn't funny. At least it wouldn't be if the man ended up with a smashed-in skull. Which he didn't actually think was very likely. "Ashley, give me the bat." He kept one eye on the woman and one eye on the man who'd managed to get to his feet. "And you, what's your name?"

"His name is fu—"

"Okay, okay." Gabe looked pointedly at the woman. "I get it. He's no good."

"Hey! I—"

"You're not!"

"Ashley, give me the bat." He now stood between the couple. "Now." She did as she was told and Gabe took the bat in hand before he turned to the man. "As for you…"

"Ryan."

"Ryan," Gabe repeated. "Why don't you come with me and I'll take you home."

"This is my—"

"This is *not* your home!"

The situation wasn't going to be easily defused. At least not while everyone was still so heated. Gabe also knew that unless something had changed dramatically since the last time he'd visited Ashley in a somewhat similar situation, it was *not* Ryan's home. At least not legally. "Is there somewhere you can stay, Ryan? At least until the two of you can talk about this with calmer heads?"

The other man nodded. "Blackwood Ranch. I'm a friend of Brian's. I'm doing some work for him."

Brian Blackwood ran a ranch just outside town. He was a nice guy, especially for a wolf shifter, but Gabe did question some of the company he kept. Or, more specifically, some of the ranch hands he hired. "Okay." Gabe gestured to his cruiser. "Get in. I'll run you up to the ranch." He waited until the man did as he was told before looking back to Ashley and handing her bat back. "As for you, you really need to start making some better choices in your personal life, don't you think?"

For the first time, Ashley looked something other than mad. She wiped at her face in an effort not to cry. "I'm trying, Gabe. I am. I really thought Ryan was different. I actually think I might be in love with him."

"Well, maybe she was his sister?" Gabe shrugged. The last

thing he wanted to do was get in the middle of whatever was going on, but he couldn't help but have a soft spot for the woman. It wasn't her fault that her taste in men was astonishingly bad.

This was the second wolf shifter he'd escorted from her house. Not that Ashley knew that. As a human, she had no idea that so many shifters lived among her in town. But for whatever reason, she seemed to have a radar for the *dogs*.

Obviously she'd actually liked this one. Gabe gave her one last encouraging smile before he got back in his cruiser to deposit Ryan out on the ranch, where hopefully he wouldn't cause too much more trouble. Maybe if Ashley tried dating a bear shifter, things would work out differently for her. Not that he was signing up for the job. He had enough on his plate for casual dating and nothing about Ashley was casual, even if she were his type. Which she was not.

No, he'd stick to what he did best.

Work.

And home.

Simple. Just the way he liked it.

IN THE LAST YEAR, everything had changed. Zoe barely recognized herself somedays, and she'd had time to get used to the new version of Zoe. No wonder Chloe was freaking out.

And she *was* freaking out.

Zoe kept her smile pasted to her face, but her eyes narrowed in challenge at her sister, who, despite her outward appearance of staying calm and collected, was no doubt losing it just beneath the surface. Zoe knew Chloe well, and she definitely knew that ever since she'd shown up on the ridge twenty-four hours ago, her sister was working double time to figure out what was going on. It also didn't hurt that Zoe had overheard

Chloe and Luke, her mate, talking earlier that morning when they thought they were alone.

"I've been out here." Zoe waved her arm around to encompass the beautiful forest.

"Don't get smart with me." Chloe crossed her arms and widened her stance. "You know exactly what I mean. Where have you been, Zoe? Mom and Dad have been freaking out."

She sighed and let her head drop back. "I'm sure they haven't been *freaking out*." She used her fingers to make air quotes. "I just took a little trip. I needed some space."

"Space?" Chloe jerked her head in the direction of the lodge and the buildings. "Let's go back to the Den so you can tell me about it."

"I really don't want to talk about it." And she didn't. But Zoe followed Chloe anyway. There really was no point in arguing too much. After all, she needed a place to stay and it had been her decision to seek Chloe out in her new home at the ridge. She probably shouldn't be too hostile.

They walked in silence for a few minutes and Zoe was beginning to think Chloe had actually respected her decision not to talk. But as soon as the buildings came into view, Chloe turned to face her on the trail. Her face had softened, and so she no longer looked pissed off, but that wasn't going to sway Zoe's decision to talk. Not yet.

"Look, Zoe." Chloe reached out and took her hand in hers. "I don't know what's going on, but Mom and Dad seem to think you're having some sort of breakdown."

"I'm not. I just wanted—"

"I know." Chloe cut her off and gave her a smile. "I know you're not having a breakdown. But you do have to admit, your behavior is a little out of the ordinary." She didn't wait for a response. "But I'm glad you're here," Chloe continued. "I really am. And you're welcome to stay at the ridge as long as you need to."

"Really?"

Chloe nodded. "Of course. And I'm not even going to make you talk." She tilted her head and added, "At least not yet." *Of course.* "But I want you to know that I'm here if you want to. Because obviously—"

"Seriously, Chloe."

"Okay." She dropped her hand. "But I am going to call Mom and—"

"No." Zoe froze and crossed her arms tight across her chest. "You're not going to call them."

"Yes." Chloe faced off with her. "I am. They need to know."

"They don't need to know anything." She didn't mean to, but Zoe struggled to control her voice. Her bear raged just below the surface. Over the last few months, she'd done a pretty good job at controlling her bear, but there were still times when her emotions got the best of her.

Which was why it was easier to stay away from anyone who was going to push her too hard. "I mean it, Chloe." She stared at her sister, willing her to understand and stop pushing. "Don't tell them anything."

"Zoe. That's not fair."

"No." She shook her head and, without another look, took off running toward the Den and more specifically, her motorbike.

"Zoe!" Chloe was hot on her heels but Zoe already had her keys out of her pocket. The helmet was strapped on the back, and she shoved it on her head before throwing one leg over and firing up the bike.

She'd already started out of the yard, but stopped in front of Chloe, who stood on the pathway with her arms crossed, her face red with the effort of running, and probably anger, too.

"Don't make me regret coming here, Chloe." She pleaded

with her eyes to her sister, who once upon a time used to be her best friend. Would she still, after all these years, feel a loyalty toward her baby sister? "Please."

Zoe didn't wait for Chloe to answer before revving the engine and taking off down the twisty mountain road that would take her into town, and with any luck, something—or *someone*—to distract her.

Chapter Two

IT HADN'T TAKEN long to drop the wolf off at Blackwood Ranch. The way he always did, Gabe gave the man a pep talk about women and how they could be temperamental. He refrained from asking whether Ashley was right, and Ryan *had* cheated on her. Beyond wanting the best for the woman he didn't really know all that well, it was none of his business.

They'd sort it out together.

Or, it wouldn't be long before Gabe was paying them both another visit.

He was just about to drive away, when Gabe noticed a familiar truck parked farther down the yard, closer to the stables. It belonged to Grizzly Ridge and the Jackson brothers who lived at the property next door. With his hand up as a visor against the sun, it wasn't hard to spot Kade Jackson, the youngest of the brothers, leaning up against the fence, chatting with Brian Blackwood.

It was Brian who spotted him first and waved him over.

"Don't tell me one of my guys got into trouble again." Brian shook Gabe's hand heartily in greeting. "Not that I don't like to see you, man. But…"

"Just a minor domestic." Gabe turned and gave Kade a slap on the back man hug before tucking his thumbs into his belt. "Nothing major. Ashley Morris—"

Brian groaned. "Which of them is messed up with Ashley this time?"

"Ryan," Gabe confessed. "But I actually think she likes this one. It could work out."

"Yeah, right." Brian rolled his eyes.

Kade chuckled. "Maybe you should pick some better ranch hands, Blackwood?"

"Not all of us are so lucky to have a shit ton of family members to work for free, Jackson." It was friendly ribbing, but there was an undercurrent of truth there as well, and maybe even resentment. The relations between the two families hadn't always been so friendly. Mostly it had been a misunderstanding with one of the Blackwood cousins, but Gabe still wondered whether the two families weren't just one more misunderstanding from a feud. That was the thing between wolf shifters and bear shifters. It wasn't often that two alpha clans could live in such close proximity without it turning out badly for at least one of the families.

"Well, either way," Gabe jumped in. "I hope Ashley gets some better taste in men sometime soon."

"Ahh, but then you'd be out of a job." Kade punched him good-naturedly in the arm.

"Somehow I doubt that, with the way things are growing around here. You guys both look like you're booming." Gabe didn't even have to look around to see that all the horses that were usually in the stables were currently out on trail rides. The full parking lot already told him that Blackwood Ranch was likely at capacity for guests. And Grizzly Ridge had been almost fully booked since the day they opened as Montana's newest eco-lodge, just over a year ago.

"We can barely keep up," Kade said. "Not that I'm

complaining," he added quickly. "But we seem to have almost as many people staying on as leaving. It's putting a bit of a cramp on our accommodations."

"Which is why he's here." Brian laughed. "Not that I can give you too many rooms, Jackson. Not even for family. At least not once the busier winter season starts up."

Gabe looked between the men. "Who do you have staying on at the ridge?" And before Kade could answer, Gabe added, "Besides Harper's mom and—"

"Nina and Ryker?" He laughed but he shook his head. Only two weeks earlier, Kade's oldest brother Axel had gotten married to Harper, which wasn't usually a shifter tradition, but seeing that Harper was a half breed, the wedding was important to her. And to her mother, Shelly, who'd made it to the ridge for the celebrations. It turned out that Shelly wasn't in a hurry to leave, though, especially because she'd had the chance to meet her brand-new granddaughter.

"That's right," Gabe said. "I forgot about Nina and Ryker. But aren't they building themselves a cabin?"

"Isn't everyone?"

"You guys are going to run out of woods over there, if you keep building cabins." Brian crossed his arms and grinned, but Kade wasn't laughing.

"Can't turn away family, man."

Ryker was cousin to the Jackson brothers, and an alpha in his own right who, like his cousins, had left his overbearing grandfather and happily settled on Grizzly Ridge with his new —human—mate, Nina. The Jackson patriarch had old-fashioned views about how his grandchildren should be choosing their mates, and considering none of them had chosen what he would consider an acceptable match, they'd all chosen exile. At least it was working out pretty well for them.

Unlike Gabe's own, self-imposed, exile from his own clan. Not that it was working out *poorly*. It was just…well, it just was.

But it never failed to make him a little homesick for his own clan and something that never was, when he saw the way the Jacksons stuck together.

"But it's not just them." Kade was still talking. "Now it seems like we have even more *guests*. Chloe's sister showed up out of the blue the other night." He shook his head and laughed. "I don't know much about her yet, but I'm not going to lie—it's pretty funny to see the way Chloe gets fired up when she's around."

The men stood around bullshitting for another few minutes before Gabe finally made his exit. His shift was almost over, and it would be good to do one more sweep of Main Street before signing off for the night.

"I'll see you guys in a few days for the citizen's patrol meeting. And you're helping out at Halloween?"

With the town growing so quickly that the police force was having trouble keeping up, it had been Gabe's idea to employ a group of volunteers from the community to help out with some of the more basic issues around town. An idea both the town and the townspeople had jumped all over.

"Absolutely."

"See you soon, Wilder."

The sun was starting to set as Gabe made his way down the lane and off the ranch. He stopped the cruiser on the drive to adjust the visor. But when he dropped it down, a photograph fell to his lap and he immediately flinched. He held the picture in two fingers and silently cursed himself. He'd meant to tuck it back into his wallet after the last time he'd looked at it.

Without thinking, he moved to fold it along the worn crease and do just that, but something stopped him.

He liked hanging out with the Jacksons, but there was part of being their friend that sometimes got a little harder than it should. In the last year, all the brothers, and now the cousins, were pairing up and falling in love. But not just falling in love. They were finding their mates. Their *fated* mates.

Gabe looked at the picture and stroked over the image of the brown-haired girl in it with his thumb. He'd had that once. Sometimes it felt like a million years ago. And, in some respects, it was.

He no longer kissed the picture the way he used to. Time changed things. Instead, he turned it over and his face split into a smile at the image of the toddler, a younger version of him, held in his arms as the three of them posed for what would be their last portrait as a family four years ago.

Ashton.

His son was no longer so little, but he still had Gabe's heart. Completely.

He was just about to tuck the photo away safely when a flurry of dust and gravel whipped past on the dirt road in front of him.

"What the hell?"

Instinct kicked in as Gabe flipped on the lights and sirens and, with the photo tossed to the seat next to him, put the cruiser into gear and tore after the reckless driver.

So much for a slow shift.

WHO DID *Chloe think she was? She was a grown adult. Her parents did not need to know where she was every second of every day.*

Zoe revved the engine, and kicked the shifter, changing the gear on her bike as she pressed down on the throttle. Speed. She needed speed. Craved it. The rush of danger she felt every time she rounded a tight corner, almost laying the bike down before once again shifting the gears and hitting the gas, made her feel alive.

She wasn't always a thrill seeker. In fact, the old Zoe would never have gotten on the back of a motorbike, let alone driven one as fast as she did now.

But the old Zoe was long gone, left behind in a cloud of dust and gravel, just like the life she thought she'd have. And good riddance, as far as Zoe was concerned. Because the way she lived now was exactly what she should have been doing all along.

Moving from town to town, finding one new adventure after another, trying new things, meeting new people, pushing the bounds of safety straight into the danger zone: *that* was living.

The mountain road that led from Grizzly Ridge down to town was twisty and tight, but that only made her speed up. By the time Zoe saw the flashing lights and heard the siren behind her, it was already way too late.

Shit.

The last thing she needed was a ticket. Chloe would definitely have something to say about that.

Zoe eased her hand off the throttle and slowed the bike. She was almost off the dirt road and into town, so she navigated the bike easily down the road before pulling over safely on the pavement at the edge of town.

It only took a few minutes before she heard the sound of a car door slamming shut and the distinctive footsteps behind her. Her senses were always on high alert after she'd been riding. She could see, hear, and scent things much more strongly. And there was a scent in the air, too. Something besides the thick, fresh pine that filled the air in the Montana mountains. Something...different.

Cedar and...oranges?

Every cell in her body vibrated, but somehow she managed to stay upright and wait for the officer.

"Ma'am?"

Zoe turned to the voice and immediately was hit with a

shock wave of desire. The man in front of her was tall and built, with hard muscles that were evident even through his uniform. The stubble on his chin, not quite enough for a beard, but just enough to look dangerously sexy, matched his black, thick hair. His dark sunglasses hid his eyes. Unfortunately, or maybe fortunately, because Zoe was pretty sure she'd be lost if she could only see his eyes. It was clear that he was a bear. Even if she hadn't been able to scent it, he had the look.

"Do you know why I pulled you over?"

It took Zoe a moment to realize he was speaking. His thick, gruff voice, every bit as sexy as the man who stood in front of her, put every one of her senses on high alert.

She took a breath, trying not to inhale, and answered. "I'm sure it was because I'm a woman on a motorbike."

He opened and closed his mouth, clearly not expecting her answer. "No," he said after a moment. "I assure you, that was not the reason. You were speeding, ma'am. On the ridge road."

Slowly, Zoe unhooked the buckle on her helmet and removed it. In doing so, she shook her long blonde hair out so it fluttered over her shoulders. She knew exactly the effect it had on men. It never failed. And when she finally snuck a look over at the officer, it was clear that her technique wasn't going to fail her this time either. "I'm really sorry if you thought I was driving too fast, Officer…"

"Wilder. And you *were* driving too fast." He stiffened his spine and stood straight once again. "License and registration, please."

The smile fell from her face. "What?"

"License and registration, please."

"But, I…" She let the words trail away. It wasn't as if she could tell him that her flirting had never failed to work before. Even when that female cop pulled her over in Idaho, she'd batted her eyelashes a little and *accidentally* undone a button on her blouse, and she was given a warning to slow down. There was no way it wouldn't work with this guy. Especially because…well, she couldn't put her finger on it. But there was something about him.

But maybe he didn't feel it.

Zoe turned away and opened the small console where she should have kept her registration. She fumbled with a stack of papers for a moment before dropping them. "Oops." She shrugged as casually as she could before bending down to retrieve them, and popped a button of her blouse at the same time. When she righted herself, she flung her thick hair back and pressed her chest forward. She knew her purple lacy bra would be peeking out. Not enough to be slutty, but just enough to be enticing.

It's not that she liked using her sexuality for her benefit, but she liked to think of it as a tool in her kit. Besides, if it worked, why not use it? Especially because she'd left her purse with her driver's license in it and her updated registration back at Grizzly Ridge.

"Here you go." She slipped her sunglasses off and batted her eyelashes at him as she handed him a stack of papers that was most definitely not her registration or her license, but he barely looked at her.

"What's this?"

"What do you think it is?"

He shook his head. "It looks like a stack of coupons for burgers and fries."

She shrugged but he still wasn't looking up.

"I'll need to see your license and registration, please."

It was no longer just lust, or attraction, or whatever it was that was racing through every one of her senses; it was also anger. *Who the hell did he think he was not to notice her?*

She was being petulant and she knew it. But Zoe couldn't

seem to stop herself. Of course, she had been looking for trouble. Maybe this was exactly what she was looking for.

"Look, Officer." She licked her lips in one last effort. "I don't have them on me right now."

For the first time, he took his glasses off and made eye contact. The second his gaze connected with hers, it was as if someone had taken a match and lit a fire. The heat was instant and intense and it threatened to knock her off the bike altogether.

WHY HAD HE DONE THAT?

He should have kept his glasses on. He knew that. From the moment he'd pulled her over and approached the bike, he'd known. She smelled of jasmine, cherries, and...*trouble*.

And if his bear had reacted as strongly as it had before she even said a word, then when she opened her mouth to speak, his bear went into full animal mode. He was lost. He was also smart enough to know exactly what an attraction so intense meant.

He needed to hold it together. Which was exactly why he never should have taken his sunglasses off. It was bad enough she was flirting shamelessly. Licking her lips, batting her eyelashes, and...*fuck*—that cleavage. It made him want to do things to her that he had absolutely no business thinking of during a traffic stop.

But the second he made eye contact, he was a goner.

Shit.

"Ma'am." It was a Herculean effort to control his voice when his bear was so close to the surface. "I'll need you to get off the bike."

So I can bend you over it and—

No! He could not afford to lose control. Not now.

If she recognized what was going on with him, it didn't show. Not that Gabe was in any way fit to identify what was going on with her—the woman whose name he still didn't know—when he could barely control his animal.

All he knew was she was a bear of some kind, and his instincts had kicked into overdrive.

Pull it together, man.

She did as he asked, and lifted first one leg and then the other from the bike until she stood directly in front of him. "Officer, I don't—"

"Call me Gabe." *Why had he just said that?* He needed to maintain some sort of professionalism or he'd be completely lost.

"Gabe." *Was he imagining things or did her voice have an extra little lilt in it when she said his name?* Either way, he loved the way she said it. "Have I done something wrong?"

She'd lowered her eyelids and was very obviously making an effort to flirt her way out of whatever trouble she might be in. It would have worked, too. If he'd been any other officer in Jackson Valley. Hell, it might even work with him. Especially if he couldn't keep his animal under control for at least another ten minutes.

"Yes," he said slowly. "If you can't produce your paperwork, ma'am, I'll need to—"

"I'm afraid I don't have them on me right now, Off—Gabe." She winked this time as she said his name. "I was in kind of a hurry to get away from my sister and I'm afraid I left my purse back at the ridge with my license and my new registration papers."

"Grizzly Ridge?"

Her gorgeous face lit up with a bright smile. "You know it?"

Gabe nodded once. "I do. The Jacksons are friends of mine."

She jumped up and down a little and as much as he knew he shouldn't, Gabe couldn't help noticing the way her breasts bounced, only barely contained in her blouse. *Damn.* She was special. Curvy in all the right places. She wore tall black leather boots that hugged her strong calves, and her tight jeans showcased full hips and an ass he'd love to get both his hands on. She was shorter than him, and the height difference gave him the perfect vantage point to take in her ample bosom that strained her blouse, her nipples hard beneath the thin fabric, either from the cool October day, or...*attraction?*

"So you must know Luke? He's my sister's mate. But I don't know how he puts up with her. I mean, she's always—"

"You're Chloe's sister." It wasn't a question, he remembered Kade mentioning that she'd shown up.

"Yes." She tilted her head and stared at him. "You've heard of me?"

"Word travels fast." He shrugged. "Small town."

"So does that mean you're going to let me go with a warning?" At once, her flirty tone was back. She took another step closer to him until she was literally only inches away from touching him. His bear roared and when he looked down once again to see her chest heaving with every breath, he came closer than he ever had before to completely losing control.

Gabe clenched his teeth and shut his eyes against the vision of her breasts and the urge to rip the next tiny button from her blouse so he could cup his hands around each perfect swell to feel the heft of them. He knew they'd fit as if they'd been custom made just for him. *He knew it.*

Finally, he took a breath and opened his eyes. It was a force of will, but Gabe took a step backward to put distance between them. "I will give you a warning," he said. "This time. But I—"

"Thank you."

Before Gabe realized what was happening, she had her arms around him and was squeezing him in a hug. He knew how he was *supposed* to handle situations like this. He'd been caught up in more than a few awkward moments when women wanted to thank him for something or another. So, yes, he knew he was supposed to delicately extract himself from the embrace, take a step backward and move on with his day.

But knowing what he was supposed to do versus what he wanted to do were two very different things. Which was why, before he could stop himself, he had a hand on either side of her head and kissed her thoroughly.

Chapter Three

"GOOD MORNING."

Zoe lifted her head from the counter to see Luke, her sister's mate, walk into the kitchen. She raised a hand in a show of a wave and dropped her head down again.

"Don't tell me you slept in the kitchen?"

"I wish." Reluctantly, she sat up and propped her head up with her arm.

"You wish you'd slept in the kitchen?" Luke poured a cup of coffee and slid it over the counter to her. "You don't like the bed upstairs? I've never heard any guest complaints about the accommodations."

"No, no." She pulled the coffee close and inhaled deeply. "It's not that at all. The room is gorgeous. Thank you. And thank you for this." She lifted the mug. "And of course for letting me stay."

"Of course." Luke pulled up a stool of his own and sat across from her. "So why couldn't you sleep in our gorgeous room?"

"It wasn't the room." She sipped the coffee. It was hot and

just the right amount of bitter. Perfect. "I just couldn't sleep. At all. It was like the worst case of insomnia ever. And I've never even had insomnia." Zoe dropped her head in her arms again on the counter. She'd tried everything the night before, but her brain would just not shut off long enough for sleep to take over.

It had never happened before. Ever.

"Any idea what was keeping you up?" Luke looked genuinely concerned. Everything about her sister's mate was genuine. Zoe had only known him a few days, but she couldn't help but be impressed with her sister's choice. Luke Jackson was a perfect mate for Chloe. Which Zoe couldn't help but secretly laugh at because her older sister had always openly declared how she'd never settle down with a mate.

"I have no idea," Zoe lied. "I could just cry I'm so tired." She dragged her cup closer and sat up again.

"Well, don't do that." Luke pushed up from his stool. "If Chloe thought I'd made her little sister cry, she'd be pissed. And I do not need one crying female and another pissed-off one." He laughed. "No thanks."

"I hardly think Chloe would care." Focusing on her sisterly relations would be a good distraction. And way easier than letting herself think about the reason she couldn't fall asleep the night before. "It's not like she's cared about my life since she left home."

"That's not fair." Luke looked over at her from where he stood at the fridge. "She cares about you. A lot. And I know she's worried about why you've shown up here so suddenly."

Zoe lowered her gaze and exhaled slowly.

"Your parents are worried about you, Zoe. Chloe too."

"I suppose she's going to call them and let them know I'm here." She sounded like a petulant brat and she knew it but she couldn't seem to stop herself.

Luke shook his head. "She wants to." He took a carton of eggs from the fridge as well as various other ingredients and put them on the counter in front of her. "But I convinced her to wait," he added unexpectedly. "At least for now. You're a grown woman and from what I can tell, you don't seem to be in any danger of any kind. Omelet?" He gestured at the supplies as he grabbed a bowl.

"Sure." She sat up straight and reassessed him. "You convinced her not to call?"

He nodded. "Surprised?"

"I am." Zoe crossed her arms over her chest while she watched him get to work preparing breakfast. "Why would you do that?"

"Like I said." Luke stopped, egg in hand, and looked her straight in the eye. "You're a grown woman. And the way I look at it, we all have our own demons. Yours made you run." She opened her mouth to object, but he continued to talk. "I also know that the ridge has a way of helping people come to grips with whatever it is that's haunting them. I think your time here will be good for you."

Zoe dropped her arms and stared at him.

"Am I wrong?"

She shook her head slowly and let a small smile creep across her face as an image of her sexy police bear flashed in her mind. If she closed her eyes, she could still feel the heat of his lips on hers, the way he'd twisted his fingers through her long hair and held her close as their mouths explored the other. It was, without a doubt, a kiss unlike any other she'd ever experienced. And her bear had instantly gone wild with the taste of him.

Zoe had no idea how long they'd stood there on the side of the road, lost in each other. It wasn't until a car drove by with a little honk that they'd come apart. The look on Gabe's face, equal parts stunned and turned on, no doubt mirrored hers and Zoe knew if they weren't careful, things could escalate between them, and fast.

Which was why she'd grabbed her helmet, popped it back on her head, and without another word, fired up her bike and taken off down the road. She drove far enough to put some distance between them, but still her instincts were in overdrive. She got off her bike and once more took her helmet off in an effort to take a deep breath and cool down.

Damn. Their connection was hot. No, beyond hot. It was absolutely on fire, and it wasn't as if she wouldn't enjoy a little romp with a sexy grizzly shifter. Given the way her body was vibrating, every nerve ending firing all at the same time, she'd definitely like to get him alone…and naked.

But that type of attraction could be dangerous. *Very* dangerous. Especially if her hunch was right, and it was more than lust.

Maybe Luke was right and her time at the ridge would be good for her. But maybe, if she was right about Gabe, it would only serve to destroy her.

There was only one way to find out.

THAT KISS.

It was all Gabe could think of.

Everything about kissing a stranger during a routine traffic stop was wrong. *Very* wrong. He knew that. He also knew that he could face disciplinary action for it. He also knew he didn't give a shit.

What he didn't know was her first name.

Not that it mattered. At least not for the moment. Because everything about that kiss had been—

"Dad! You're not listening."

Gabe blinked and shook his head until the image of the curvy beauty who'd had his bear roaring faded away, replaced by his reality, which was brought sharply back into focus.

"Sorry, kiddo." He turned to Ashton, who perched on a stool at the counter next to him, a bag of chocolate chips in hand. "What were you saying?"

"I asked if I could put the whole bag in." His six-year-old son grinned. He was no fool and he knew when his dad was distracted. Unfortunately for him, Gabe was on to him.

"No deal, kid. Half a cup, just like the recipe says." He handed Ashton the stack of measuring cups. "Can you find the right cup? It has a one with a two under it. That means it's half."

With a sigh, Ashton put the bag down and began his search for the right measuring cup. After a moment, he triumphantly pulled it from the stack and Gabe let him measure in the proper amount.

When he was done, he took the bag and held it out to his son. "Don't forget the good luck chips."

"The what?"

"Good luck chips." He dipped his hand into the bag and pinched a few chocolate chips with his fingers. "Reach in and grab a few. Not too many," he added with a wink. "Then before you throw them in the batter, you make a wish. Ready?" Next to him, Ashton reached into the bag and nodded seriously. "Okay," Gabe continued. "Make your wish and when you're ready, toss them in like so." With a flourish, Gabe shot the chocolate bits into the bowl. A moment later, Ashton did the same thing.

"Did you make a wish, kiddo?"

Ashton nodded seriously. "Yup. Did you?"

Gabe smiled and ruffled his son's hair. He always made the

same wish: that his son would grow up happy and healthy. So far, so good. As a single dad, it wasn't always easy, especially because Ashton didn't even remember his mother. He was only a toddler when the crash claimed Marie's life and that of their unborn child. In the first few years after the accident, Gabe was sure it was a blessing that his son didn't have to deal with the same crippling grief that he was experiencing. But now that time had lessened that grief, leaving mostly memories that made him smile, Gabe had started to believe it was a cruel unfairness that meant Ashton would never remember the woman who'd loved him more than anything else in the world.

"I wished for a—"

"Whoa." Gabe held up a hand. "You can't tell me. It won't come true. You have to keep it a secret."

Ashton grinned and made an elaborate show of zipping up his mouth and locking it and Gabe couldn't help but laugh.

"Let's get these cookies on a sheet and in the oven," he said. "You can take them to Grandma's tonight."

"Can we have cookies for dinner?"

Gabe gave him a pointed look although he knew there was a good chance that with his mother-in-law in charge, there was no doubt that Ashton would have at least one cookie *after* he had a healthy dinner. They were lucky to have Maryann, Marie's mom, so involved in their life and Gabe knew it. His own parents weren't really the warm, cuddly grandparent type and after the accident, they'd only become colder toward him —if it were possible. There was only so many times you could listen to your parents tell you how disappointed they were in you because you'd been driving the car that went off the road, killing your wife. As if it ever needed to be said.

It was an accident.

One he lived with every day.

Which was why, as soon as he could, Gabe packed up what was left of his family and moved to Boulder Creek, a tiny town in the middle of Montana where Marie's mom had settled after her daughter's death.

It had been the best thing he could have done.

A fresh start for both of them.

A chance to build a life.

And find a mate?

The thought, along with the image of the blonde-haired beauty—Chloe's sister—took over his senses. *A mate?* He had a mate.

Correction. He'd *had* a mate.

He'd loved Marie. She was a fantastic mate and mother. They had a life together. A *great* life.

But was it fated?

Gabe had never once questioned his relationship with Marie and what they shared together. But in recent months, he'd watched his friends the Jacksons fall in love, one by one, with their fated mates. And that seemed different in a way he couldn't quite put his finger on.

He'd never felt the same type of draw to Marie that his friends had with their mates. The same intensity that they all seemed to share. Not that he hadn't loved her.

Of course he had.

Damn.

Guilt flooded him the way it always did when he thought about Marie and the life they'd had together. The last thing he wanted to do was sully her memory in any way. She'd been his mate and he'd loved her.

"Dad, I'm going to go get my Transformers."

Automatically, Gabe nodded. "I'll get these in the oven."

He used the few minutes of quiet to refocus. Gabe prided himself on being a hands-on dad despite all the help he got from Maryann. When he was with Ashton, he liked to stay present with him and made it a point not to look at his phone when they were spending time together or be distracted by anything else. *Including thoughts of blonde-haired beauties.*

"DON'T RUN AWAY AGAIN." Chloe's voice stopped Zoe moments before she did just that.

Not that she was really going to run away. Just head out for a run on the ridge. It was a gorgeous day, and now that she had some coffee in her, she was more than ready to get moving.

"Please," her sister added when Zoe moved to put her hand on the door. "I think that's the least you could do."

With a sigh, she turned around and flipped her hair off her face. "I don't want to fight with you, Chloe. I really don't."

Her big sister smiled and immediately Zoe had the urge to go to her and let Chloe soothe her the way she had so many times before when they were kids.

But they weren't kids anymore and not even Chloe would be able to soothe away the hurts in her soul this time.

"Will you come for a walk with me?"

Zoe nodded. "I was actually going to go for a run."

Chloe grabbed her coat and joined her at the door. "Sounds good. But let's talk first."

She nodded, even though it was the last thing Zoe really wanted to do. She couldn't put it off forever, though. So she might as well get it over with.

They walked in silence until they were away from the main buildings and were finally alone on a trail. Despite the fact that it was already the second week of October, it was sunny and warm, with only the slightest chill in the air. Zoe hadn't brought a coat with her. No need considering she was planning to shift and go for a run, but Chloe didn't seem to be in any kind of hurry to let her run.

They walked a bit farther before finally Zoe couldn't take the quiet. "What do you need to know, Chloe?"

"It's going to be like that, is it?"

Zoe stopped short. "Like what? You said you wanted to talk, so—"

"Enough." Chloe turned and put her hands on her hips. "I've had enough of this spoiled rotten, wounded little girl act." Zoe tried not to, but she couldn't help but react to her sister's anger. Chloe almost never spoke to her that way. "You came *here*, remember? You've been missing for months, Mom and Dad have no idea where you are, and all of a sudden, you show up on my doorstep, acting like nothing's wrong but you refuse to talk about it?" She shook her head. "I don't think so. At the very least, you owe me an explanation, Zoe, and you know it. So talk."

Her first reaction was to say something sassy and put her off. But Zoe swallowed hard and dropped her head for a moment. She'd been running for a few months now, and despite what she'd hoped when she'd first taken off on her bike, her problems were no further behind her. And they never would be.

"Okay."

"Okay?"

Zoe nodded. "I didn't mean to worry anyone, Chloe. Really." She hadn't. Her leaving had nothing to do with anyone else. Only her. She'd needed space and she told her sister so.

"But why? This isn't like you." They sat together on a fallen log and Zoe picked at a patch of dried moss. "Me, maybe." She smiled. "But not you. You were never the rebellious one. You were always the—"

"Good one?"

That made Chloe laugh. "Well, I wouldn't say that you were the *good* one." She used air quotes. "But yes, you were definitely the daughter who would have been voted least likely to have a nervous breakdown of any kind."

It was Zoe's turn to laugh, but only for a minute. "Do you remember how when we were kids I was the one who couldn't wait to grow up, find my mate, and live happily ever after, having as many cubs as I could?"

Chloe nodded. "I remember it well. I never could understand that. It was the last thing I wanted for my life." She shrugged at the obvious irony. The only thing missing from Chloe's life now was cubs, but that couldn't be too far off either. "Are you saying that you don't want that anymore?"

"No." She shook her head sadly and much to her frustration, tears sprang up in her eyes. "That's the problem." Her voice was small as she looked up at her big sister. "I do want it. Badly."

Despite the distance and the wall Zoe had successfully put up, their bond was strong and Chloe didn't hesitate before she reached over, wrapped her arm around Zoe, and pulled her in for a hug. Instantly, the weight of her sister's arm had her crying in earnest. Thankfully, Chloe didn't say anything but just let her cry. Much to Zoe's surprise, it felt good to get the tears out. Of course, she'd cried before, but not since she'd left home.

There was no time for crying when you were constantly on the move. Town to town, meeting new people, getting into all the trouble she'd avoided when she was younger…there was little room for tears.

After a few minutes, her tears slowed and only then did Chloe stroke her hair and say, "Hey. Why don't you tell me what's going on?"

Zoe sat up, wiped her face, and turned to her sister. "I can't want that anymore because I can't have it."

Chloe shook her head. "That doesn't make sense. Why

can't you have it? Are Mom and Dad forcing you to mate with—"

"No." It wasn't unusual in the clans to have rules about who you could mate with, but the Karringtons had never been like that. They'd even let Chloe, their oldest, go off to school and then take a job traveling as a way to *avoid* finding a mate and settling down. The irony that Chloe had actually met her mate while doing it was strong. "It's not like that," Zoe continued. "They don't even know what happened."

"So what *did* happen? Why do you think you can't find your mate?"

"That's not it and that's the whole problem, Chloe. I think I *could* find my mate." The sexy bear cop's face flashed in her head again. But she pushed thoughts of Officer Gabe away. "I mean… if I were looking, I'm sure I could find him. But I could never enter into such a union because it wouldn't be fair. That's what I'm trying to tell you." Zoe jumped off the log and took a few steps away before she turned around again. "I can never have cubs." Every time she said the words aloud, it caused a physical pain in her chest. "The doctors told me a few months ago. The chances of me having a successful pregnancy are pretty slim."

"I don't understand." Chloe shook her head. "Is it a genetic thing? How do they know?"

"It's the craziest thing." Zoe paced again. "I went for my yearly checkup and mentioned to the doctor that I haven't been having regular periods." She shrugged. "I honestly didn't think anything of it, but they ran some tests. I wasn't even worried, Chloe. I mean, why should I have been?"

"What did they say?"

"I have something called POI. Primary ovarian insufficiency. It basically means my ovaries don't work."

"What?"

"I know, right?"

"That doesn't make sense."

Zoe shrugged. "Does anything make sense?"

"So what does it mean?"

Zoe stopped pacing and looked straight at her sister. "It means the chance of me having children of my own are extremely rare. And you and I both know what that means when it comes to a mate. If I can't give him a cub…if I can't…" She let the idea drift away. "It's not fair for me to take a mate. Not ever."

Chapter Four

"BREE, WILL YOU PUSH ME?" Ashton, already a successful flirt with the ladies, batted his eyelashes in the direction of Bree Brooks, owner of Bree's Knees clothing shop in town, and most importantly, Gabe's best friend. She'd been one of the first people Gabe and Ashton had met when they'd moved. And although she was human, she seemed to know all about the shifters living among her and not only didn't have any problem with it, but considered a lot of them some of her closest friends.

"You know I will, kiddo." She left her paper cup of coffee on the picnic table where they'd been sitting and raced Ashton to the swing set. Gabe followed them with a laugh. He stood off to the side to avoid being hit by his son's wildly swinging legs as Bree pushed him higher and higher.

"So," Bree said after she got Ashton swinging high enough to squeal in delight. "Were you going to tell me about the blonde-haired woman you were kissing on the side of the road yesterday or were you waiting for me to bring it up?" She winked at him, and Gabe groaned.

"I thought it was you who drove by."

"You're lucky it was," she answered. "What was that all about? Since when do you make out with women during traffic stops?"

"I know." He shook his head. "It was stupid." *But amazing.* "I don't know what came over me." *Her intoxicating scent.* "It was the craziest thing. "I don't even know her first name."

Bree looked at him sideways.

"I mean, I know she's Chloe's sister, but—"

"It was a traffic stop," Bree interrupted. "Isn't there a whole part about license and registration?" His friend laughed, tossing her long strawberry-blonde hair back over her shoulder as she got ready for another push. Not only was she amazing with Ashton, she was sweet and kind and a successful business owner, as well as incredibly pretty. The Jackson brothers had all asked him at one point why he didn't ask Bree out on a proper date. Even Maryann had mentioned it once or twice.

But it wasn't like that with Bree. They were friends. *Best friends.* And even if he was willing to jeopardize that—which he wasn't—neither of them felt any of the attraction that was necessary for a relationship to work.

Not like the light-haired beauty on the bike.

That was a level of attraction that Gabe had never felt. Not ever. Hell, it was enough to jeopardize his job.

"She didn't have her papers on her," Gabe admitted, earning another questionable glance from Bree. "And one thing led to another and I didn't actually catch her first name."

"I should say. That was one hell of a traffic stop." Bree laughed again and this time Gabe found himself laughing along with her. "But I know who she is."

His laughter cut off abruptly. "Who?"

Before she could tell him, Ashton demanded more pushing and Bree obliged. After a few strong shoves that sent him once again soaring in the air, Bree stepped to the side and said,

"Well, you already know she's Chloe Karrington's sister." He nodded. "Her name is Zoe."

Zoe.

Kade and Brian had been talking about Chloe's sister. They had the same electric blue eyes. Even with the different hair color, he should have seen the similarity. But he'd been too busy trying to keep his bear in check to worry about physical similarities with his friend's mate.

"Zoe?" Just saying her name woke his bear up.

"Yep. She showed up out of the blue the other night," Bree continued. "As far as I know, Chloe doesn't even know why she's in town. She said something about how Zoe had kind of taken off without telling anyone and her parents were really worried. I guess it's totally unusual behavior for her. I wonder if Chloe would think that making out with a cop on the side of the road was unusual behavior?"

She was teasing, but still Gabe shook his head and clenched his jaw. "Do not say anything."

"No fair."

"What's not fair?" Ashton's swing was coasting to a stop and his little ears picked up everything lately.

"That I have to work so early tomorrow," Gabe answered and Bree rolled her eyes. "Come on," he said. "Let's get going so I can get you to your grandma's. You get to sleep over tonight and she'll take you to school in the morning because I'll be working the graveyard shift. Sound good?"

"Yup." Ashton nodded the way Gabe knew he would. He was lucky to have such an easygoing kid.

The three of them chatted about Ashton's class and some of his favorite classmates as they walked along the street. Gabe couldn't help it as his gaze drifted toward the end of the road where he'd met Zoe. His bear started to grumble, his instincts on alert as they got closer. But it wasn't the spot in the road that his bear was reacting to.

As the threesome made their way a little farther down the street, the scent of fresh cherries filled his senses. *Zoe.* Without thinking, Gabe turned toward the Station pub and sure enough, there was the motorbike. He took three steps across the street before Ashton's voice stopped him.

"Dad. Where are you going?"

He froze and turned around, still standing in the middle of the street. Bree watched him with raised eyebrows. No doubt she knew exactly where he was going.

"I just saw that there was a new flyer on the community message board." It was a lame excuse, but it was all he could come up with. Gabe jogged across the road and grabbed the flyer before holding it up triumphantly. "A fall festival." He looked at Bree, who'd grabbed Ashton's hand and joined him on the other side of the street. "What fall festival? Do you know anything about this?"

Bree shrugged. "The Jacksons were talking about doing something as a thank-you to the town for being so accepting of them and the lodge. I guess they decided on a fall festival. Can I see?"

Gabe handed Bree the paper.

"Pumpkin carving, archery, bobbing for apples, hay rides, and more," she read. "Sounds fun."

"Totally!" Ashton bounced up and down. "Can we go, Dad?"

Gabe looked to Bree in question.

"It's this Saturday," she replied. "From one to nine. There's going to be a bonfire as well."

A chance to visit Grizzly Ridge, and Zoe? He wouldn't miss it. "Of course." He grinned at his son, who did a fist pump in the air. "But that's still almost a week away. And right now, we need to get you to your grandmother's so I can catch a nap before my shift."

Bree leaned in and whispered in his ear so Ashton wouldn't hear. "A nap? Or maybe a stop in at the pub?"

Gabe stared at her. *How could she know?* "It's not like that."

His best friend laughed. "Yeah, right."

She was right. It had taken a great deal of restraint to walk away from the Station pub and the scent of cherries that filled the air, but there was no way he was going to be able to go in. Not with Ashton with him. Besides, even if he did go see her, what would he say?

It wasn't about what he would *say* so much as what he would *do*. And Gabe knew it. The next time he saw Zoe, he knew he'd have to taste her again. Only this time, he wasn't so sure he'd be able to stop at only just one taste.

***

AFTER HER TALK WITH CHLOE, Zoe was wrung out and she'd needed to get away. Not that it hadn't felt good to come clean with her sister. It had. But it had also brought up all of the feelings she'd been trying to run away from. And there was no point to dwell on any of that. Especially when there was nothing she could do about it.

Even Chloe hadn't known what to say. That was because there was nothing *to* say. Nothing at all.

So instead of hanging around and letting herself think about it, Zoe had joined Ella and Harper, who were making up flyers for a fall festival that the Jacksons had fairly spontaneously decided to host. They only had one week to take care of the details and let everyone in town know about it. Zoe had taken the stack of photo-copies and offered to put them up around town. Which she'd done.

Her task had taken her right past the Station pub, and considering she'd done such a good job, and had worked up a thirst, she didn't see any problem with stopping in. And with any luck, she'd be able to find somebody to take her mind off her troubles. Or even better, she could get into some trouble. *Maybe with a sexy bear cop?*

She was still laughing at herself when she walked into the dimly lit pub and took a seat at the polished wooden bar. She turned on her stool and scanned her surroundings. There wasn't much in the way of other patrons so early in the afternoon, but a few guys were seated farther down the bar. *Humans.* A big guy seated alone in a booth. *He was all grizzly.* But brooding and moody. She didn't want anything to do with that. In the far corner of the room was her best option for a little fun: two men downing beers and egging each other on in what looked to be a very poorly played game of pool. They were shifters, but not bears. She watched, waited, and paid attention.

Wolves.

Yes, that could be a lot of fun.

She ordered three shots of tequila before making her way over to the men. Zoe didn't have a lot of experience with wolves. There weren't any in the town she grew up in, and she'd only run into them once or twice in her travels. And of course Nash, Kira Jackson's mate at Grizzly Ridge, was a wolf. But other than that, she didn't know what to expect.

With any luck, they'd be up for a bit of competition.

"You guys looking for a challenge?" She held out the shots and flipped her hair off her shoulder with her free hand. She knew she looked good. Her blouse was unbuttoned just enough to reveal the low-cut camisole beneath, along with the generous swell of her breasts. Her jeans were tight and her leather boots tall, which only accented her shapely legs. She had curves in all the right places, and judging by the men's response, they were appreciated.

"I think we are." The first one answered and took a shot

from her. "The name's Brian," he said. "Brian Blackwood. I own the ranch up the road."

"Next to Grizzly Ridge?"

"That's the one." He grinned at her. "You must be Chloe's sister."

Zoe did her best not to look disappointed that he knew who she was. Hopefully it wouldn't affect his willingness to play. "Small towns." She shrugged.

"That's the truth." Brian chuckled. "This is Gord. He works for me up on the ranch."

Zoe handed him a shot. "Wanna play?" She winked at them and raised her glass in the air. The men followed suit and they all downed their shots before Brian grabbed the triangle to rack the balls.

"Shall we make it interesting?"

Zoe chose a cue from the rack on the wall and chalked the end. "Absolutely." She gave him a sly smile. "Fifty?"

"How about a hundred?"

"Oh no!" Zoe pretended to look shocked. "I could never risk that kind of money on a game. I mean, I'm not very good."

Brian laughed. If he knew he was being hustled, he was being a good sport about it. "Sure you can." He pulled the triangle from the balls and waved toward her, giving her the go ahead to take the first shot. "I'm not very good either." He winked and Zoe couldn't help but laugh.

"Sure." She shook her head and took her spot at the end of the table. "A hundred dollars it is." Slowly, she bent at the waist and pulled her hair to one side before raising her cue and lining it up with the white ball. She inhaled slowly before making the shot.

The solid blue and green ball both landed in pockets off the break.

"Impressive." Brian whistled.

"Hustler," the other man said, but Zoe ignored him and took the next shot.

She missed.

Growing up, her family had a pool table in their basement and Zoe had gotten pretty good at the game. She knew she could probably beat both men, and if she were anywhere else, in any other town, she'd hustle them both for as much money as she could get out of them. But she was in Boulder Creek, and this guy obviously knew her sister. There was nothing to be gained from taking him for a few hundred dollars.

Except a little danger.

The thought actually appealed, but as she watched Brian sink his next two shots before missing, something else much more appealing presented itself.

Oranges and cedar.

The scent filled her. Her bear growled within. And she missed her shot, the cue scraping the side of the ball before jamming into the felt on the table top.

"Whoa." Brian laughed. "If you're trying to prove that you're not a shark, you don't need to go quite that far."

She blushed, embarrassed at her blatant slip. Even when she was trying not to play well, she'd never missed quite so badly. But she couldn't dwell on it, because her instincts were raging out of control.

Gabe. He was there.

She didn't even need to turn to know he stood in the bar, watching her. But she couldn't have stopped herself if she'd tried. And she didn't.

GABE PROBABLY SHOULD HAVE GONE straight home after dropping Ashton off at Maryann's. He should have gone to catch a few hours of sleep and a quick shower before his shift started. It would be a long night. He should have at the very least stayed far away from the Station pub.

But there was a big difference between what he *should* do and what he *wanted* to do. And his common sense was no match for his bear, who made a beeline directly back down the street and into the pub.

His senses filled with cherries and jasmine the moment he stepped inside of the dingy bar, which was a miracle in of itself considering the pub had never smelled of anything besides peanuts and stale beer in the entire time Gabe had lived in town. His eyes found her immediately and locked on the sight of her round ass as she bent over to take her shot at the pool table.

Brian Blackwood leaned against the opposite wall, watching Zoe. He had a perfect view of her cleavage, an opportunity he was taking full advantage of, judging by the look on his face. The other wolf, a man Gabe didn't know, had his beady eyes on Zoe's ass. His tongue slipped from his lips and Gabe's bear roared.

It took all the control he had to keep his bear under wraps. It wouldn't do any good to start a fight. Not here. Not like this. He was a police officer. He needed to remember that.

Besides, the men hadn't done anything wrong.

Except leer at my mate.

The thought slammed into him, but Gabe didn't even bother to correct himself. Was she his mate?

Yes. His bear roared. *Hell yes.*

While he watched, she slipped and missed her shot.

She knows I'm here.

Gabe smiled and waited. Just as he knew she would, she turned around.

She was breathing hard, her chest rising and falling, straining at the small camisole she wore under her blouse. She licked her lips, and Gabe's cock stiffened in his jeans.

Damn. The kiss the day before hadn't been enough. *Not. Even. Close.*

Mixed in with her intoxicating scent was the new and deliciously subtle scent of Zoe's arousal.

Yes. She wanted him just as much as he wanted her.

He walked toward her, their eyes locked on each other. The rest of the bar and its patrons faded away around them. He reached out to grab her arm and pull her to his lips again, to crush her mouth to his and taste all of her. Hell, he'd take her right there on the pool table if that's what it took. He couldn't think straight. He couldn't think past tasting her, touching her. Having her.

"Are we going to finish this or what?"

Brian's voice broke the spell that bound them, and Zoe turned to look in his direction.

Fuck.

"What was that, Wilder?"

Had he spoken out loud?

Gabe's focus snapped over to Brian Blackwood, who looked at him with a smug look on his face. They were friends, but Gabe would not hesitate to drop him if he got between him and Zoe. Of that there was no doubt.

"I just said, fuck that." Gabe looked right at Brian when he spoke. "Looks like it isn't much of a game anyway."

Brian took a step away from the wall. "There's a hundred dollars on this game."

If Gabe hadn't been so clouded by the presence of Zoe and the need he had for her charging through his veins, he might have been able to tell that Brian was just screwing with him. But as it was, every word of Brian's just put him further away from his goal: *Zoe.*

"I'll take my shot."

Both men turned to Zoe, who'd bent to line up her shot.

Gabe's eyes went straight to her cleavage and his vision all but blacked out. He needed her.

"Oh, yeah you will," the other man leered.

Without thinking about it, Gabe spun and grabbed the man by the neck. He had him pinned against the wall in a flash. "Don't you ever speak to my *mate* that way. And do not even think about looking at her again. Do I make myself clear?"

The man squirmed and despite Gabe's tight grip, managed a nod before Gabe released him. He turned to see Zoe staring at him, wide-eyed, her sensuous lips parted in question. Next to her, Brian Blackwood shook his head and tried not to laugh.

"I think we're good here," Gabe said. "Yes?"

"I'm good." Brian was fully laughing now. "We can finish the game another time."

Zoe nodded, but didn't take her eyes off Gabe, who'd reached out a hand. She took it and immediately heat flared through him. But also a sense of something else.

Home.

Zoe felt right. It was crazy. It didn't make any sense at all and Gabe couldn't even begin to understand it. But as he led Zoe through the bar and outside, he didn't spare a thought for *making sense* or *understanding* anything. It didn't matter.

The only thing that did matter was having this woman in his arms, taking her mouth with his. And the moment they were in the fresh air, he pushed her against the brick wall of the building, and that's exactly what he did.

Chapter Five

ON SOME LEVEL, Zoe knew she should probably protest being pulled out of the bar as if she didn't have a say in what was happening. After all, she was not some weak woman who could be bossed around.

But the moment Gabe pushed her up against the brick wall and started to kiss her, any and all thoughts of putting a stop to what was happening dissolved like mist around them.

Besides, she was far from weak. She had the power to drive a man so completely crazy that he could barely complete a sentence, he was so driven to distraction by her.

But not any man.

Her man.

A groan escaped her at the involuntary thought because despite herself, it felt so damn right. Gabe was her man. Her *mate*. And she knew it with every fiber of her body.

"God, you're sexy." He pulled his mouth away from hers long enough to mutter the words. But a moment later, he was kissing her neck, his hands moving over her body as if he couldn't get enough.

She certainly couldn't. Zoe's own hands grabbed at his T-shirt, pulling at the cotton fabric, desperate to pull it over his head so she could see the smooth muscles she knew it was hiding. "Gabe, I need you to—"

"No." He stopped, his hand on her breast, and she almost screamed. "We can't do this here."

Why the hell not? As far as Zoe was concerned, they could do absolutely anything and everything right where they stood because there was no way she was going to be able to go anywhere else, not if it meant waiting to have him. She would completely self-combust.

Thoughts of Gabe had completely consumed her since they'd met the day before. And when he'd walked into the bar, his presence filling every single one of her senses, Zoe knew she was going to be completely lost to him. She'd never before felt anything even remotely like the sensations that ripped through her right now, which meant only one thing.

And her bear already knew it.

Gabe was her mate.

And dammit if that didn't both excite her and scare the hell out of her all at the same time. She meant what she'd said to Chloe. When she got the news from the doctor, Zoe had promised herself she'd never allow herself, no matter how tempted, to take a mate. But that sure as hell wasn't going to stop her from *having* him.

Sex and mating were two *very* different things. And as far as Zoe was concerned, you could deny yourself only one of those things.

The other…was hers for the taking.

At least, if her bear had anything to say about it.

"Yes," she whispered roughly into his ear. "We can." She bit down on the sensitive skin on the base of his neck and he groaned as his hips pressed her harder into the wall.

Yes. They could definitely do it here.

But a moment later, Gabe pulled back with a grunt

although he held fast to her hand. "Come with me." She felt the loss of his body against hers almost immediately, but somehow her feet moved as Gabe pulled her to the back of the building and out of sight of Main Street. "I can't do what I want to do to you in the middle of the street."

"And what is it you want to do to me?" She grinned and tugged on his arm so he had no choice but to kiss her again. A situation that she was more than happy to be in.

He growled. "So much."

They still were fairly out in the open, but at least no one was likely to walk by. A row of thick trees blocked them from the alleyway beyond, and unless someone came out the back door of the pub—which they could easily do—they weren't likely to be discovered. At least, not *as* likely.

"Zoe, we probably shouldn't do this here." Much to her frustration, Gabe pulled back again. "Someone could see."

"Exactly." She licked her lips. "And how did you know my first name? Been asking around about me?"

He nodded slightly, his eyes heavy with desire. "Something like that."

She reached out and grabbed him by the belt, yanking him forward while at the same time undoing the buckle.

"Zoe…"

"You worry too much." She tugged down the zipper and slipped a hand inside. As her fingers wrapped around his thick length, she groaned and closed her eyes. "But not all of you is worried." Zoe looked up and challenged him with her eyes. "You want me."

"No." He shook his head. "I *need* you."

———

THERE WERE SO many reasons that Gabe should stop. So many reasons he should force himself to move slower.

. . .

THEY WERE IN PUBLIC.

Anyone could walk by and see them.

He actually liked her. Maybe it could turn into something?

He'd never moved so fast before.

He wasn't that kind of guy.

She was his mate.

But with Zoe's hand on his cock, squeezing and stroking, Gabe couldn't think of any of those reasons—even if he wanted to.

Which he didn't.

He tugged her thin camisole down and lifted her breasts from the lacy constraints of her bra. They were heavy and full with hard pink nipples that stood hard at attention. Gabe growled as he sucked one into his mouth while he pinched the other, just enough to elicit a groan. Zoe arched her back and pressed into him. As much as he wanted to get to know every inch of her body, there was no time.

His cock throbbed in his jeans.

He used his hands to undo her pants, her hands still occupied with him, and she shimmied until they slid down to her ankles.

"Are you...do you..." He could barely get the words out, but he needed to be safe. Even in the throes of lust, he wasn't completely irresponsible.

"It's fine." Her words came out as a pant. "I'm fine."

He kissed her again. Hard. And she met him with an equal ferocity. "Damn, woman."

She grinned against his mouth.

Gabe pulled his lips from her, and with one hand spun her around so she was pressed against the brick wall. She groaned and pushed her bare ass back to him. He reached around with one hand and cupped her breast. With his other hand, he braced himself as he slid from behind into her wet heat.

She made a noise somewhere between a moan and a growl when he entered her. The sensation of being inside her was everything. It was both familiar and completely uncharted. Gabe gave himself a moment, wanting to go slow and enjoy every second of her, but Zoe wasn't having it.

She pushed backward, grinding herself against him. He responded by squeezing her breast before thrusting once more into her.

"Oh...my..."

"Fuck." Gabe's bear was only barely beneath the surface. He'd had the slightest taste of her, but he wanted more. He had to force himself to stay in the moment and keep control over his animal.

It didn't take long before he could feel his climax building from the base of his toes. Beneath him, Zoe started to shake. Her body trembled as her own orgasm crested. He pinched her nipple and she cried out, exploding around him. A moment later, he took his own orgasm, his bear roaring in pleasure.

God, this woman.

He'd never done anything like that before. Not even close. And Gabe had no idea how to respond to what they'd just done.

Reluctantly, he pulled back and Zoe turned around. Her eyes were heavy with lust, the grin on her face the sexiest thing he'd ever seen. Her chest heaved as she struggled to bring her breath back to normal. He couldn't take his eyes off her.

"That was..." She shook her head and licked her lips.

After a moment, Gabe collected himself enough to shake his head. "I've never...I don't do—"

"You don't do that kind of thing," she finished for him. Zoe tugged her shirt back into place and bent down to pull her jeans up. She reached behind her and pulled her hair over one shoulder. "Like you don't fuck strange women in alleys?"

Her words stopped him, but it was her cold detachment that made him take a step back. "That's not what that was."

"Isn't it?" She tossed her head to the side and turned to walk away.

Gabe moved quickly to do up his jeans and go after her.

He caught up to her as she was turning the corner around the building. Gabe reached out and grabbed her arm, pulling her back and spinning her around. He pushed her up against the wall and kissed her again. "No," he said after a moment. Zoe's breath was coming fast and he caged her in with his arms, unwilling to release her until she understood that *no*, what they did was not just a one-off. "It wasn't about fucking a strange woman in the alley." He looked straight into her green eyes and he could see the understanding reflected back to him. "And you damn well know it."

Chapter Six

AFTER HER TRYST with Gabe behind the Station pub, Zoe spent the rest of the week up at Grizzly Ridge. It was safer to stay hidden from the world than to risk running into him again. And it would be a risk, too, because clearly the two of them could not handle being in the same space without wanting to tear each other's clothes off.

Normally she'd be perfectly okay with that. Particularly because the chemistry between the two of them was completely off the charts. For the whole week after they'd had sex, Zoe couldn't stop replaying it in her head. And damn, it was a hot image. The way he'd turned her around and taken her from behind. She couldn't remember sex feeling that phenomenal. Not. Even. Close.

But nothing about the situation was normal. And as much as she'd quite happily replay the scenario in real life, it was too dangerous. *Way* too dangerous. Because the crazy, erotic feelings that continually crashed into her when she least expected it, like when she was helping with the dishes earlier—or worse, when she was helping stack hay bales in the yard for the fall festival and had to excuse herself to go for a little walk before she made herself climax just reliving the scene—those weren't even the dangerous feelings.

No. What was dangerous was that the feelings Zoe was having for Gabe weren't all sexual.

If they were, that would be *way* easier.

Because the feelings she was having about Gabe that made her want to stay home on Friday nights cuddling under a blanket, sharing a bowl of popcorn before spending the rest of the weekend holding hands and doing home repairs like the happy couple she could actually envision herself being with him —*those* were scaring the hell out of her.

Which was why she was just going to stay up at Grizzly Ridge, hiding from the world until she figured out where she was going to go next. Because it was clear that she couldn't stay at the ridge forever and she definitely couldn't go down to Boulder Creek again. No way could she go to town. Not with a certain sexy cop patrolling the streets. Not when the pull toward him was so strong that it almost caused a physical ache inside her.

She had to focus on something, anything else. With a sigh, Zoe grabbed a stack of tablecloths that were stacked and ready to go outside. She'd been helping out in the Den, which was serving as headquarters for the festival activities. Everyone buzzed around with excitement for the last-minute fall festival the Jacksons had decided to put on. It was happening that afternoon, but there was still so much to do and get organized. Ella and Kira, both heavy with pregnancy, were doing a lot of the planning and *supervising* from inside. Zoe couldn't help but be impressed with how well the two of them could organize everyone else. More than that, how well they all worked as a team.

That was probably because they were all fated mates. They were all so in sync, that everything just ran like a well-oiled machine at the ridge. The idea that Zoe would never have that for herself made her inexplicably sad.

Maybe hanging out at the ridge was a bad idea.

"I'm going to take these," Zoe said to no one in particular before pushing her way outside with the stack of tablecloths.

The cool air helped to clear her head a little. What she really needed was a run along the ridge and through the trees, but there was work to be done and she'd committed to helping.

The run would have to wait.

"Hey, Zoe," Nina called out to her with a wave across the field where she was setting up tables with another woman she didn't recognize. "Bring those over here."

Nina was fun and easygoing and was also a new arrival to the ridge, not that Zoe considered herself an *arrival*. Her presence was temporary. But still…

"You must be Zoe." Nina's friend greeted her with a smile and a wink. "I've heard so much about you."

What had she heard?

"I'm Bree," the woman continued and held out a hand. "A good friend of Gabe Wilder's."

Oh, that explained it.

Sort of.

Zoe looked to Nina, but if the other woman knew anything about what had gone down between her and the friendly cop, she wasn't giving anything away. The question was, how much did Bree know? Not that it really mattered. It wasn't as if there was ever going to be a *relationship* between them. And he didn't seem like the type to kiss and tell.

"It's nice to meet you." Zoe shook the woman's hand. "I don't really know Gabe that well." She didn't know why she felt the need to explain anything to this woman, but she couldn't seem to stop herself. "I mean, he seems like a nice guy."

"He's the best." Bree nodded but didn't seem to expect her to say anything more, a fact Zoe was grateful for.

"Can you give us a hand with these tablecloths, Zoe?" Nina started to unfold one, and handed her an edge before waiting for a response. "After this, we're almost done and people are expected to start arriving in about an hour." Nina continued a steady line of chatter. "Has Harper or Kira given you a job yet?"

Zoe shook her head. Apart from helping out with whatever needed to be done, she hadn't been assigned anything.

"Well, I think the plan is to have some stations set up for the kids," Nina continued. "I offered to do apple bobbing and Bree is doing face painting."

"As long as they don't go sticking their head in a bucket of water after I paint masterpieces on their cheeks." Bree laughed.

"I think there's an archery station," Nina offered. "And some ax throwing."

"Ax throwing?" Zoe's mouth fell open. "I'm no expert but is it really a good idea to let kids throw axes?"

The ladies laughed. "The axes are for the adults," Nina said. "And the arrows in the archery station have suction cups on them for the kids. No worries about shooting anyone's eye out."

"Well, what fun is that?" Zoe shook her head and laughed. "Kidding," she added quickly. "I think archery sounds like something I can handle. I'll go check it out."

What she really wanted to do was take off and hide in the woods for the next few hours. After all, what if Gabe showed up at the ridge? How was she going to control herself around him in front of so many people? Her instincts were running wild and her bear was only barely under control when he *wasn't* around. It was as if she were a teenager with wild hormones raging through her all over again. Only what she was feeling for Gabe was far from a teenage crush.

Maybe helping kids shoot arrows at a target for a few hours would be a good way to forget about Gabe and the feelings he brought out in her. Besides, if Gabe did show up to the festival, he was far more likely to be drinking beers with the Jackson brothers or throwing axes than hanging out with the kiddie games.

Or maybe not. But at this point, she'd try anything.

ZOE.

Taking Zoe against the wall. Feeling her heat. The way her entire body had shuddered with need. His bear roaring with satisfaction.

For the last six days, Gabe had tried—and failed—to think of anything but Zoe and their short time together.

Hell, he didn't know anything about the woman.

Except that she was his.

She was his mate.

His bear knew that without a doubt. And that was all he needed to know.

From the moment she'd ridden into his life, just over a week ago, Gabe's bear had roared to life in a way that he didn't even think was possible anymore. When Marie died, he'd been so sure his bear had died with her. He'd loved her so completely. How could it be possible to love again?

But Zoe was different. His bear had reacted completely different with her than it had ever reacted before. Even with Marie.

The pull toward Zoe was one he couldn't fend off. It was too strong. Their connection too intense.

Part of him had hoped that after they'd had sex he might get her out of his system a little bit, but the exact opposite had happened. Now, instead of simply thinking about the woman all the time, he was completely consumed by her.

Unless he concentrated with all of his energy, everyday tasks were almost impossible to complete. It was only with a Herculean effort that Gabe could focus on work. And when he was with Ashton, he had to focus specifically on his son, because the moment he let his mind wander, thoughts of Zoe slammed into him without warning and completely took over.

He couldn't keep going this way. Something was going to have to be done.

Especially because Captain Williams, his old police chief from back home, had called the day before to deliver a message. Billy Benson was appealing his case again, and they might need Gabe to speak at the hearing. He needed to concentrate. He needed focus because there was no way in hell he was going to let Billy Benson get out of jail. He'd immediately pulled his old file and started to review his notes.

As if he even really had to. Gabe knew that he'd be able to recall every detail of Billy Benson's case until the day he died. The moment Gabe had answered the call for a domestic assault at that red brick single story, his life had been changed. It was only six months after Marie's accident, and he'd only just gone back to work in an effort to distract himself.

He'd responded to the call, only two hours into his shift. It had been a neighbor who'd placed the call, and it was clear, judging by the way Billy's wife Darla cried in the corner, unwilling to talk to Gabe, that she wasn't about to press any charges. It was also clear that it wasn't the first time Billy, a mountain lion shifter, had hit her.

Gabe had left that call feeling helpless. Sure, he'd taken Billy in for drunken misconduct—which had only pissed him off more, and there was nothing like pissing off an already angry cat—but they all knew he'd only be able to hold him for twenty-four hours and then he'd be back in the home, wreaking more havoc and potentially ruining more lives. It made Gabe crazy. But it continued to happen. Almost as if Billy knew how much it angered Gabe that he couldn't arrest him if Darla didn't press charges, Billy upped his game and soon Gabe answered more calls at their house than ever before.

He knew it was only a matter of time before the man killed his wife. Fresh off the grief of his own loss, there was no way Gabe could let that happen. Which was why he'd finally tracked Darla down at the grocery store where she worked for minimum wage. Darla had likely been a pretty woman once. Probably long before she met Billy. And it wasn't just the bruising and swelling that had aged the woman. It was the stress and worry that had been ingrained in her face, the sense of desperation and acceptance that her life wouldn't ever get any better, that had turned Darla into an old woman long before her time.

Gabe went back to visit Darla four times over the course of two months before he finally convinced her that he would be able to protect her if she pressed charges against her husband. To this day, he didn't know what it was that had changed her mind, but she finally agreed to press charges. Gabe had Captain Williams's consent and cooperation to keep Darla safe, and he was on his way over to her house to collect her when he'd gotten the call over the radio.

He was too late.

Billy, drunk again, had picked a fight with Darla; Darla, feeling emboldened by her recent decision, must have made the choice to tell him that she was going to press charges and send him to jail. To this day, Gabe didn't believe that he'd actually meant to kill her. But an angry cat was unpredictable. Even to his own self. Billy had lashed out—drunk, and out of control, his claws had sliced Darla's throat.

When Gabe showed up, Billy was sitting on the kitchen

floor, his wife's lifeless head in his lap, fire in his eyes and blame in his heart.

That was just over three years ago. Three years that Gabe regretted every day not being able to save the woman. And three years that Billy had sat in a prison, convinced his mate's death was Gabe Wilder's fault.

But that would all change if Billy Benson was able to successfully appeal his case. He'd be released until the new trial and he'd made no secret about the fact that if he was released, he would come after Gabe. In fact, for the first six months that Billy had been locked up, Gabe had received three letters threatening exactly that. He'd turned them in to the authorities, who'd assured Gabe they'd put them in Billy's file. Which was why it was more ludicrous that they could even consider reassessing his case.

If Billy Benson was on the streets, he was dangerous. Not only to his own family, but to Gabe and his. And that included Zoe. Because she *was* his. And even if he didn't need his instincts to be sharp—which he did—he needed to make her his.

Now.

He needed to see her. He needed to talk to her.

He needed to mate her.

Gabe knew that was the only answer yet it seemed too crazy. They'd only just met.

He pulled his truck up to Maryann's house and took a deep, cleansing breath as he got out to stand on the sidewalk.

"First things first, Wilder," he said aloud. "Go talk to her. Get to know her." He nodded as he spoke aloud to himself. "Yes. That's what I need to do. Simple. No problem."

"Dad?"

Gabe spun around at the sound of Ashton's voice.

"Who are you talking to?"

Gabe ruffled his son's hair as he joined him on the front lawn. "Myself," he answered honestly.

Ashton wrinkled his nose and shook his head. "Why would you talk to yourself? That's silly."

"Not at all," Gabe said as seriously as he could. "Turns out I'm a good listener." Ashton rolled his eyes, and Gabe laughed. "Are you ready to go to the festival?"

"Yes!" The little boy jumped up and down. "Grandma said there'd be candy apples."

"Did she, now?" Gabe looked past his son to the doorstep, where his mother-in-law stood with a tea towel in her hands and a smile on her face.

Maryann shrugged at Gabe's comment. "What's a festival without candy apples, right?"

He laughed and walked toward the woman. Ashton had spent the night again because Gabe had the graveyard shift. "Thanks again for watching Ashton last night," he said as he got closer. "You know how much I appreciate it."

"And you know how much I love you both." She waved away his gratitude. "You don't have to thank me, you know that. And you know I'm always happy to have Ashton, even if you want to go out socially."

Something in her tone grabbed Gabe's attention. "What are you talking about?"

Maryann wiggled her eyebrows and laughed. In that moment, she looked younger than her years, not that she was terribly old. But life had dealt her some harsh blows, and they'd taken their toll on the strong grizzly shifter. She'd lost her own mate when Marie was only a child and had never dated again. Gabe knew it wasn't for lack of offers. Marie used to tell him about her mother's suiters, and how she turned each of them down. There was always a hint of sadness in her eyes that Gabe attributed to that loss, and when Marie died, that sadness had only grown.

It wasn't often Gabe saw a lighter side of his mother-in-law. And he was certain he'd never seen her wiggle her eyebrows before. He tilted his head in question and waited.

"I'm not saying anything," she said, only barely controlling her laughter. "Except, a little birdie may have told me that there's a blonde female in town who may have caught your attention."

Damn small towns.

Gabe shook his head out of reflex. "Maryann, it's not like that." It was a lie and they both knew it.

"Stop." She held up a hand. "You don't have to explain anything to me. Marie is gone," she continued softly. "You're not doing anything wrong."

"But I'm not doing—"

"Gabe," she interrupted before he could lie to her again. "It's okay. And I, for one, think it's a good thing. You're a young man. You need to live your life. You don't do anyone any good pretending otherwise. Now go to the festival and have fun."

Thankful for a change of topic, Gabe jumped on it. "I don't know why you don't come with us. You'd enjoy it, Maryann. It would do you some—"

"Don't you tell me what's good for me." Her look chastised him and he smiled with a chuckle. "Not unless it involves a long bath, a glass of wine, and a good book. Because that's what's waiting for me this afternoon."

"Fair enough." He waved and turned to leave. But before he did, Gabe turned back one more time. "Thank you, Maryann. For everything."

She nodded because they both knew he was thanking her for a whole lot more than just watching his son.

"OKAY," Zoe said to the little blonde-haired girl. "Now you lift it up in this arm, and carefully look down the arrow. Good. Just like that. And when you're ready, you—yes! Good job." She turned and gave the girl a high five when she hit the target.

Zoe had been at the archery station for over an hour and was having a much better time than she'd expected. The children were all excited and turned out to be quick learners. Whether they hit the target or not, she let them pick a little prize from a basket of small toys Harper had given her to hand out.

She let the little girl try again before letting her choose a toy and moving on to the next kid. "Your turn," Zoe said to a little dark-haired boy who stood alone in the line. "Are you ready?"

The boy nodded. "Yup."

"Great." Zoe gestured him into position and handed him the bow. "What's your name?"

"I'm Ashton," the boy said confidently. "I'm six and my dad says I can be anything I want."

Zoe giggled. "I bet you can. And what do you want to be?"

"Robin Hood."

Zoe had to swallow down her laughter because the boy looked so serious about what his future goals were. "Well, I think I can maybe help you get a little bit closer to that goal," she said. "Have you ever shot an arrow?" She felt an unusual draw to the child. She liked all the children she'd interacted with that day, but there was something different about Ashton. Special.

Ashton nodded. "My dad showed me once."

"Awesome. So you already know what to do?"

Ashton nodded again and his dark hair flopped over his forehead. He brushed it away and Zoe caught a glimpse of his light-gray eyes. They were unusual, yet also familiar. But she didn't have time to think about where she'd seen eyes that color before because Ashton was lifting the bow and drawing it back. He seemed quite confident, so she let him do his thing, and sure enough, when he released the bowstring, the arrow flew straight and true across the distance, where it landed with a satisfying smack against the target, the suction cup planted firmly on the bull's-eye.

"Great shot!"

The little boy looked at Zoe with a grin, proud of his shot.

"You're pretty good at that. Do you want to pick a prize from the basket?"

Of course the answer was yes, and Ashton selected a temporary tattoo before thanking her and running off to the next activity.

She watched after him for a minute and allowed her mind to drift the way she almost never let it.

What if he were my son?

What would *her* son look like if she had one? It was a game she used to play before she found out about her infertility. It used to be fun. A game of *what-ifs* and *maybes* and picturing the future. But lately, it was a game of heartache, and one she no longer allowed herself to play.

But something about Ashton had Zoe breaking her own rule. She watched him as he went over to where Chloe handed out candy apples. Even from the distance, Zoe could see the way his eyes grew wide at the treat in his hand.

As he wandered over to the lineup for the wagon rides, Zoe made herself look away. There was only so much she could take. But now she was agitated, and with no more children waiting to try their hand at archery, she started to look for something else.

Or someone else.

No. She couldn't let herself think about Gabe. The festival had been a good distraction and maybe with a little luck she'd be able to get through the rest of the day without making herself crazy with thoughts of him.

She turned in a half circle until she saw Nina's mate, Ryker, and Kade across the lawn with axes and a large wood target.

Perfect.

"Can I give that a shot?" she asked as she walked up to the men.

"Absolutely." Ryker handed her a hatchet, and kept the large ax for himself. She glanced between the small hatchet and the ax and rolled her eyes. "What?" Ryker said. "You want this one?" He lifted the heavier ax.

"Of course." She traded him tools and easily swung it over her shoulder. She might be a smaller, black bear to his alpha grizzly, but that didn't mean she wasn't perfectly capable of handling the big ax.

Kade shook his head and chuckled. "Ryker, man, you should know better."

Zoe grinned and lifted the ax, planted her feet, and took aim. With a grunt, she hefted the heavy steel into the air and watched as it rotated over and over before lodging into the target.

A sense of satisfaction washed through her as the blade dug into the wood.

"Nice work." Ryker whistled appreciatively and jogged over to retrieve it. "Wanna try again?"

"Damn straight."

She threw the ax three more times, each time the satisfaction of the blade biting into the wood calming her bear a little more than the last. She lifted it one final time, and pulled it back behind her head, ready to feel the burn in her muscles as she hurled it toward the target. *Maybe she should have taken up ax throwing a long time ago? Hell, she wasn't even thinking of—Gabe?*

The ax left her fingers at the exact moment that the scent of cedar and orange overwhelmed her senses. *He was here.*

"What the hell?"

"Watch out!"

The men yelled, and a moment later, there was a shriek, followed by someone else yelling her name. But to Zoe, it was all background noise, because the only thing she could focus on was Gabe standing next to the horse-drawn wagon covered in hay, staring directly at her. With a little dark-haired boy holding his hand.

GABE PROBABLY SHOULD HAVE REACTED. He should have run over to make sure that the ax that Zoe had just wildly thrown hadn't hit anyone. But he couldn't move. The moment she turned and locked eyes with his, he was frozen to the spot. His instincts had gone haywire to the point that he was no longer in control of basic bodily movements like speaking or moving.

"Dad." Ashton tugged on his arm. "That's the one."

Belatedly, Gabe realized Ashton had been trying to get his attention. He really had to get it together. He shook his head roughly and ordered his bear to calm the fuck down. *How was he supposed to function at all if every time he saw the woman he basically shut down?*

"What's that, Ash?" He crouched next to his son, forcing himself to look away from her. "What's the one?"

"The woman," Ashton repeated himself. "That's the woman who had the bow and arrow. She's the one I told you about. That I liked. She feels…"

"She feels what?" Gabe didn't want to push him, but somehow, whatever his son was about to say felt very important. "What does she feel like?"

Ashton blinked, his long dark lashes standing out sharply

65

against his freckled skin. He looked up and right into Gabe's eyes when he said, "Home. She feels like home."

Whatever Gabe was expecting him to say, it wasn't that. He caught himself moments before falling over. He got to his feet quickly so Ashton wouldn't see his reaction.

Was it possible that his son could feel a connection to Zoe's bear, too? Was it fated?

It had to be. There was no other explanation.

He looked over to the ax-throwing area and the chaos that had erupted there when Zoe had seen him. There was no doubt he had an effect on her, too. And it was time they figured out just exactly what it was. Gabe grabbed Ashton's hand. "Why don't we go say hi?"

A moment later, they stood in front of her and it was all Gabe could do to keep from grabbing her and pulling her into him, kissing her until they were both breathing the same breath, and never letting her go. Ashton's hand wrapped tightly in his rooted him to the present.

"Hi."

She blinked and looked between him and Ashton. "Hi." She spoke the word to Ashton. "Is this your dad?"

Ashton nodded and her face lit up with a smile that came from somewhere deep inside her. Slowly, she looked up and met his eyes. "You're a very good teacher, Gabe. Your son got a bull's-eye on his first try." Her eyes searched his and he knew instinctively that she was saying *Why didn't you tell me you had a child?*

I didn't have the chance, was the answer he tried to convey to her.

"Do you want to get some apple cider with us?" he asked instead. "You made quite an impression on my son."

For a moment, she looked as though she were going to refuse. No doubt she was having the same struggle with being so close together and not being able to tear each other's clothes off. Gabe's bear was almost completely out of control. It was an exercise in pure will to keep him reined in.

She nodded and looked to Ashton again. "My name is Zoe," she said. "I don't think I had a chance to introduce myself. Sorry about that."

"That's okay." He jumped the distance between them until he stood at her side, took her hand and started to lead Zoe toward the tables where Ella and Kira were serving apple cider and freshly baked cookies.

He watched as his son and the woman he was very quickly coming to realize was his fated mate walked hand in hand away from him, and not for the first time wondered what exactly he was going to do about it.

Chapter Seven

"I DIDN'T KNOW you had a son." Zoe swung her legs over the edge of the log fence she and Gabe perched on. It hadn't taken long for Ashton to finish his apple cider and run off to play with a group of kids who were currently climbing a stack of hay bales. She watched him with a mixture of confusion and awe.

"I guess we didn't really have too much time to talk before."

She probably should have blushed. But the only thing that the memory of their coupling behind the Station did was turn her on. She reached across the space between them and ran her finger along the top of his hand. "That's true." She couldn't help but laugh. It was the strangest thing, but she both felt as if she'd known Gabe for years, and also as if she'd only just met him and still had to learn so much about him.

Both were true.

"He sure seems to like you." Gabe turned and looked in her eyes and immediately something inside her melted a little. She was like a teenager in love for the first time. Only it was more than that. "And I mean," Gabe continued, "he *really* likes you. I've only ever seen him drawn to one other woman that way."

"Another besides his mother?" It was a question that needed to be asked. Although Zoe didn't sense another woman in Gabe's life, there must be. At least in some way. After all, he had a *son*. Of course, she'd been so clouded by him, that she hadn't sensed that either.

Gabe shook his head. "No. Not his mother. His grand-mother. They're very close." Before Zoe could ask any more, Gabe continued. "His mother, my mate, died when Ashton was only two. He doesn't remember her."

"I'm so sorry." She turned on the fence and grabbed Gabe's hand while she searched his face. "That must have been terrible. Poor Ashton."

"It was terrible." He nodded. "A really rough time. But it was years ago. And we're doing good."

It was ridiculous, and awful, but Zoe couldn't help but be jealous of Gabe's dead mate. *Had they been fated? Was their connection as strong as the one Zoe seemed to share with him?*

She swallowed back the question and looked straight ahead to the hay bale pile and Ashton, who now stood on the top with his arms raised over his head.

Gabe squeezed her hand until she looked at him again.

"I'm sorry." Zoe shook her head. "I really don't know what to say. I don't think I've ever met anyone like you."

"Like a widow with a small child or someone so irre-sistible?" He wiggled his eyebrows and she couldn't help but burst out laughing.

"Both."

He laughed with her for a moment and then his face grew serious. He took both of her hands and held them tightly. "For the record, Zoe…I find you completely and totally irresistible. I don't know how you feel about these things…" He gestured around them with his head. "I know there seems to be some mixed opinions around here about it, but…for what it's worth, I know this to be true. We're fated."

Fuck.

Zoe squeezed her eyes shut against his words. Not because she didn't believe him, but because she did.

"Zoe?"

She shook her head and refused to look at him.

"You don't believe?"

The hurt in his voice was too much. She snapped her eyes open. "I'm sorry," Zoe said. "I have to go. I promised I'd help with the festival and…well…" She couldn't make eye contact with him. If she did, she feared she'd never be able to look away again. "I have to go."

Without another word, she took off running.

DAMMIT.

She'd come to Grizzly Ridge to get away. To avoid everything. So why this? What kind of sick joke was it to meet the one man she knew she was fated to be with when all she'd wanted to do was hide?

Is that really true?

Her bear challenged her and she growled her disapproval under her breath.

If that was true, you would already be gone.

"Stop it!" she yelled aloud, forgetting she wasn't alone. She offered an apologetic smile to a woman she didn't recognize and kept walking. She needed to get away. Go for a run, blow off some steam. But she knew she couldn't do that either. There were too many humans around for her to shift. And even if there weren't, the last thing she needed to do was let her bear take over because clearly her animal didn't seem to agree with her on a few key points.

Like her need to stay away from Gabe.

Instead, Zoe walked as fast as she could through the middle of the festival, intent to get to her motorbike, jump on and drive away. Because the farther she got from Gabe and his son, the better.

Right?

"Zoe!"

She spun around to see Chloe surrounded by guests who were all enjoying the festival. No one seemed to notice the sisters staring at each other. Even from the distance, Zoe could see the question in Chloe's eyes. *Don't run,* she was saying. *Stay.*

Tears sprang to Zoe's eyes, and before she had a chance to swipe them away, Chloe was by her side, her arm around Zoe and steering her away, into the adventure center, the building where they kept all the mountain bikes, snowshoes, and other gear. The moment they were inside, Zoe started sobbing.

For a few minutes, Chloe didn't say a word, but simply rubbed her back and held her the way she did when they were little and Zoe came home in tears because a little boy at school had teased her. And then, just as she had when they were kids, once Zoe's tears ran dry, Chloe pulled back a little, looked her in the eyes and said, "Chin up, butter cup. Nothing's worth turning that beautiful smile upside down for."

When they were kids, Zoe would usually start laughing, wipe her tears, and tell Chloe everything. But she wasn't a kid anymore. And some things were worth the tears.

"He is," she said after a moment. "He is worth turning my smile upside down."

"Gabe?"

Stunned, Zoe took a step back and blinked hard. "How did you know?"

Chloe only laughed. "Everyone knows, Zoe. Even if half the town hadn't seen you making out on the side of the road last week, the other half can easily see the way the two of you look at each other. And I'm pretty sure every single person at the festival could feel the heat coming off the two of you a minute ago. Damn, girl, you're fated."

"No." She shook her head hard enough to whip her hair around her face. "We can't be. I already told you, I can't have a mate."

Chloe laughed again. The sound was starting to get *very* annoying. "Do you really think fate cares what kind of stupid theories you've convinced yourself of?" She didn't wait for Zoe to answer before she added, "It doesn't. When you're fated, there's a whole lot of nothing you can do about it, Zoe. I mean, you can try to ignore it, but you'll only drive yourself and everyone else crazy." She grabbed Zoe by the shoulders and shook gently. "You can't fight it, Zoe. You just can't." And then, with her voice softer than before, she added, "Why are you even trying?"

The love in her sister's voice threatened to crack her. Naively, Zoe thought she was being so strong.

A little fling with a stranger? No problem.

Some hot sex with Gabe? Yes please.

No strings attached? Absolutely not.

"I don't want to," she confessed as Chloe took her hands off her shoulders and Zoe slumped to the floor. "More than anything, I want to give in to this feeling." She dropped her head into her lap. "But I can't." She looked up into Chloe's unimpressed face. "I already told you why. I can't have cubs, Chloe. It's not fair to anyone to mate knowing that I can never give them children."

"He has a son."

"I know he…has a son," she finished slowly. "But he'd want more. Right?"

Chloe shrugged. "You don't know that."

It was true. She *didn't* know that. She'd always just kind of assumed. A question popped into her head. "Do *you* want cubs,

Chloe? Does Luke?" They seemed to be the only mated couple at the ridge who didn't have children or weren't pregnant. Except for Nina and Ryker, but they were still pretty newly mated. No doubt they'd be next.

Chloe shrugged again. "We haven't decided. Maybe. Probably. But it's not a deal breaker either way."

Zoe pushed up from the wooden floor and dusted off her jeans. "It's not?"

"No way." Her sister's grin lit up her face in a way that made her look even more gorgeous than she already was. In fact, Chloe had never looked so radiant as she did at the ridge. *With Luke.* Maybe that's what having a mate did to a woman? "I never wanted a mate, remember?"

"I do."

"So, I guess I never really gave it much thought when it came to cubs, I mean, not like you did. But now...well, you never know." She winked. "We might try. But even if we don't, I know I'll be happy with him for the rest of my life."

"But what if you can't have children?" The infertility problems she had could affect her sister, too. Was that fair? "I mean, what if you guys decide to have cubs and then you can't? You should go get tested. You should know."

Chloe shook her head and smiled. "There's no need for tests," she said. "Because it doesn't matter," Chloe said confidently. "No matter what happens, cubs or no cubs, we'll be okay."

"But you should know, Chloe."

"No. I don't need to know."

"I don't understand." Zoe shook her head and tried to look away but Chloe grabbed her hand and pulled her back.

"Zoe. You're my sister and I love you. But I think you have a lot to learn when it comes to mates. Especially fated mates. You can run and you can hide, but the love the two of you have for each other is *fated*. And in case you're not crystal-clear about what that means…" She winked and squeezed her sister's hand one more time. "It means it's stronger than any objection you can come up with," Chloe continued. "Stop fighting and enjoy it. Not everyone is as lucky as you. Besides," she added. "You'll never be able to fight it."

"YOU'RE NOT JUST GOING to sit there, are you?"

Bree's voice startled Gabe. He shook his head hard to break the stare he had focused on the adventure center building Zoe had disappeared into a few minutes earlier.

"I don't have much of a choice, do I?"

Bree laughed and sat next to him on the fence. "You do know that I'm not an idiot when it comes to your kind, right?"

"My kind?"

"Yup, the pigheaded, too stubborn for your own good, kind." She rolled her eyes. "Shifters, dummy." She smacked his arm playfully. "This isn't the first time I've seen this," Bree continued. "You can't help but learn a few things growing up in this town. And with friends like the Jacksons, well…let's just say this isn't the first time I've seen one of you *alpha grizzlies* try to deny what can't be helped."

Gabe stared at his best friend in wonder. He'd never asked how much Bree knew. She was human, but she'd lived among shifters her whole life, and was one of the Jacksons' closest friends. It was shifter code to keep the secrets of their kind to themselves. Humans should never know about their existence, let alone the details surrounding mating or how they lived. The very fact that Bree even knew about them wasn't right. But Gabe couldn't help but be thankful that she did. Because he desperately needed someone to talk to about it.

"What are you talking about?"

"Fated mates, of course."

His eyes grew wide. "What do you know about fated mates?"

She laughed and shook her head. "I know you can't fight it. You and Zoe, you're meant to be. Everyone sees it."

"Everyone?"

"Everyone." She nodded matter-of-factly. "Even you."

It wasn't a question, and Gabe didn't try to disagree. "I know."

"So what's the problem?"

What was *the problem?*

He could take the easy way out and say that the problem was Zoe and her obvious hesitancy to recognize what he—and apparently everyone else—already knew. But that wasn't fair. Because if that's all that was stopping him, it wouldn't have held him back for long. No. There was more, and they both knew it.

"I'm scared."

It wasn't often an alpha grizzly admitted to any weakness and Bree didn't bother to hide her shock. But it didn't take her long to recover. "Of what?" Before he could answer, she asked, "Is it because of Marie?"

He turned to stare at her. They hadn't often spoken of his previous mate and he knew that was mostly his fault. Gabe had no problem talking to Ashton about his mother, or even sharing memories with Maryann. But when it came to talking about their relationship, about what it had been and what they'd shared? And then, about her death? Gabe didn't want any part of that.

"No," he answered as honestly as he could. "I mean, not really. It's…" He was distracted by movement at the adventure center. The door opened, and Zoe and Chloe stepped out into the warm October afternoon. Reflexively, Gabe hopped off the fence and walked toward her.

"Gabe?" Bree called out behind him. "It's what?"

"Complicated," he tossed back over his shoulder. "Keep an eye on Ashton?"

He didn't bother waiting for a response, because he knew she would. She was a good friend, and maybe he should confide in her. But there was only one person he wanted to be talking to at that moment.

And he wasn't going to take no for an answer. Not again.

Chapter Eight

ZOE WAS ONLY a few steps out of the door when all at once her senses clouded over and she felt a hand on her arm. *Gabe.*

"Come with me." His voice was low and rough in her ear. "We need to talk."

After her conversation with Chloe, she was pretty sure that, despite her misgivings, what they really needed to do was mate and get it over with. But Gabe was probably right. His approach was a lot more responsible. They *should* talk.

She nodded and let him lead her around the building and into the woods. He didn't say a word until they'd walked for a few minutes and were far enough away from the festivities as to not be overheard.

"I can't do this anymore, Zoe."

"Do what?" It was a stupid question and they both knew it.

He kissed her hard and fast. His hand cupped her chin and held her tight to him while they satisfied their need for each other.

Only it wasn't satisfying. Not at all. She needed more. They both did.

"So what are we going to do about it?" she said, slightly out of breath. Her chest heaved with the effort to control her bear, who knew exactly what they should do about it. "I can't be your mate. It's—"

"I don't care what it is," he interrupted her. "Because you're mine and I'm yours and I know that with every single fiber in my body. And you do too."

"But, I—"

He pressed a finger to her lips. "I know you think you have a good reason to try to stop this between us, but I also know that you feel it too. We're fated, Zoe. And yes, it's crazy. We've only just met. We hardly know anything about each other. Hell, you *just* found out about my son. But none of that matters, and not only do you know it, you *feel* it. I know you do. Because it's something beyond us and completely out of our control. Because it's—"

"It's instinct," she finished for him.

"Exactly." He held her face in his huge hands and stared directly into her eyes while he spoke.

Zoe couldn't help but believe him. It *was* out of their control. And maybe it didn't matter that she couldn't have children of her own. Maybe Chloe had been right. Maybe Gabe was right, maybe…the only thing that mattered was this connection that they shared. A connection that had only driven them both completely crazy.

"You're right." She spoke before she could talk herself out of it.

"I know." His grin was so cocky and so cute Zoe couldn't help herself: she leaned forward and it was her turn to kiss *him.*

Her bear, although still wildly protesting within her, needing a release, felt oddly settled at the same time. It was the calmest her animal had been since meeting Gabe. She no longer felt as if she were going to bust out of herself. But even so, instinctively Zoe knew she'd feel a whole lot better as soon as they were mated. She needed him. *Now.*

She let her hands slide down his chest to the buckle of his jeans. There were probably a million reasons she should stop, not the least of which was that they were only a few feet away from a festival with almost the entire community in attendance. But she couldn't have stopped herself for anything. The decision had been made, and she didn't want to wait. Not one minute longer.

"Zoe, we can't…" His words drifted away as she undid his zipper and slid her hand into his jeans. Gabe's breath came out in a hot gasp as she wrapped her hand around his hard cock and squeezed.

"We can't what?"

"Not. Here." He struggled to form each word, but still Zoe didn't stop her ministrations in his pants. She wanted him and there wasn't a doubt in her mind that he wanted her just as badly.

"Yes," she countered. "Here. Now. Just like this."

A low growl came from the back of his throat before his hands locked around her hips. He picked her up easily, forcing her hand to lose its grip. He kissed her hard and lowered her to the ground. The dry leaves that covered the forest floor crunched beneath them, but despite the fact that it wasn't the most luxurious bed, it was absolutely perfect.

Gabe caged her in with his arms and hovered over her. "Like this? Here?"

She nodded, breathless and completely unable to speak.

Zoe could see the battle that waged on Gabe's face as he looked down on her.

Before he could come up with an objection that involved a soft bed surrounded by candles, a bottle of wine, rose petals, or anything else equally romantic, Zoe reached up and pulled him down to her with a kiss that told him in no uncertain terms that she didn't need any of that—she only needed him.

HE SHOULD WAIT. He should take her home and make love to her properly in his bed, where they could lay wrapped in each other's arms for the rest of the night. But there was a big difference between what he *should* do and what he *wanted* to do.

No.

What he *needed* to do.

And when she kissed him again…there was no going back.

With her lips on his, he reached for the button of her jeans. It was going to be quick and dirty. *Again.* And he longed to take his time with her, kiss up and down every inch of her and make love to her so slowly that it drove both of them to the point of distraction. But there would be time for that. Later. *Forever.*

Beneath him, Zoe groaned as he slipped his fingers into her jeans and pushed her panties aside. He already knew she was wet for him. He'd been able to smell her arousal almost since he'd arrived at Grizzly Ridge that afternoon.

"Damn, woman. You are something else."

"Yes." She traced a finger down his chest. "I really am."

A smile stretched across his face because this feisty female was all his. *Almost.*

"We're doing this?"

She nodded. "We're doing this."

If he was being logical, there were so many reasons Gabe should slow this down. He barely knew her for God's sake. And there was Ashton to think about. What would he say about having a new *mother* in his life? Hell, what would Zoe think about *being* a mother? Would she be one?

Stop thinking! Gabe's bear roared within him. His animal knew what he wanted and he was not going to take no for an answer.

Beneath him, Zoe wiggled out from under him and stood up long enough to tug her jeans off and pull her T-shirt over her head. He pulled his pants off and reached out for the naked goddess before him and silently gave thanks for the fact that he was being anything *but* logical.

Because there was no turning back.

Zoe straddled him and his hands spanned her hips as she slowly sank down onto him. Instantly, his bear was satisfied. She felt so fucking good, her wet heat around him. Zoe was everything.

A groan escaped him as she began to move on top of him. Her long, blonde hair draped over her shoulders and teased at her nipples as her breasts bounced.

"You are so fucking sexy."

She grinned and tossed her head so her hair fell behind her shoulder. In the distance, the noises of the festival reminded Gabe that as much as he wanted to, they couldn't take their time. He sat up and pulled her closer until they were pressed together. "I want you," he groaned into her ear.

"You have me."

She was so responsive, so perfect. And she was about to become his mate. Gabe kissed her neck and she moaned, arching it to give him easier access. He could feel her climax growing closer, his own, right behind.

Suddenly, Zoe's hands reached for his shirt, tugging at the hem. "I need to feel you," she breathed. "I need your skin on mine."

In a flash, he pulled his shirt off and Zoe pressed her magnificent breasts up against his bare chest.

Yes. Better.

When she kissed him again, Gabe was certain there would never be anything better than that moment.

Zoe increased her rhythm, her orgasm imminent, and Gabe shuddered as waves of pleasure started to build deep inside. "Come for me, baby." His voice was rough in her ear before he turned his attention to nipping at her neck.

Her hands pressed against his back, holding him tight to her. "*You* come for *me*," she ordered before dropping her own mouth to his shoulder, where she bit down just hard enough to send a shot of pleasure through him.

Gabe couldn't hold back any longer, which was perfect, because Zoe's own orgasm was coming hard and fast, too. His bear roared as he bit into the sensitive skin of her neck. Zoe's bear cried out her own pleasure, but the sound was muffled by Gabe's shoulder.

The orgasm that crashed through him was unlike anything he'd ever experienced. The world around them disappeared because the only thing that mattered was the two of them, and their mutual mating.

She was his.

He was hers.

Chapter Nine

THE SUN WAS STARTING to set as Zoe and Gabe made their way back to the festival. They'd dressed quickly, hardly speaking. There was an easy silence between them that hadn't been there before. As if they were both calmer, their bears satisfied. They walked hand in hand through the woods until they slipped out of the trees and came to stand next to the adventure center.

Woodsmoke and campfire filled the air. While they'd been gone, most of the activities had wound down, and most people were crowded around a huge bonfire at the other end of the property. Zoe knew there would be a s'mores station set up, and some hot dogs for roasting. Her stomach growled. She was suddenly famished.

"Hey." Gabe pulled her to him and wrapped his arms around her. "About...well...how do you feel?"

She paused with the question, not because she was unsure in anyway, but more because she had no idea how to put it into words. She let a small smile move over her face before she answered.

"Calm," she said quietly. "Calmer than I've felt in a long time. As if your bear tamed me somehow."

"Were you wild?"

His question was meant to be cute, but it stopped her for a moment. There still was so much they didn't know about each other. *Like everything.*

As if he'd sensed the sudden shift, Gabe cupped her cheek. "It's okay," he said softly. "We have time."

"Time?"

"Time to learn." He stroked her cheek. "I want to know everything about you and I want to tell you everything about me. And we will. We have time." He slipped his hand down to her neck and he brushed her thick hair aside before he used one finger to trace the mark he'd left there. "You're mine, now."

She slipped her hand under his shirt to trace the mark she'd left on him. "And you're mine."

He kissed her hard, possessively, before he said again, "We have time."

"Dad!" Ashton's high-pitched voice ripped through the bubble they'd created around them and they pulled apart. At once, Zoe missed the heat of him.

He looked to her and back to the field where Ashton had started to run toward them. Behind him was Bree.

"You should go." Zoe smiled. "Like you said, we have time."

He pressed a finger to her lips and with a wink, took off in a jog toward his son. As he reached him, Gabe lifted the boy in the air and spun him around before pulling him into a hug. She watched as he said something to Ashton that had the little boy waving to her over his dad's shoulder.

Should she join them?

Zoe hesitated. She was just as drawn to Ashton as she was to Gabe, and they were mated now. Surely that meant...what?

What did *that mean?*

Too many questions, and despite the fact that she hadn't been lying when she told Gabe she felt calmer, she couldn't help the questions that she had. Although, maybe she might be able to ignore them for a little longer.

Zoe spotted Harper over by the Den, struggling with her baby in one arm, and a large bowl in another. She gave Gabe a little wave and gestured in the direction of the Den before jogging over to help Harper.

"Let me help you with that," Zoe said as soon as she got close. She meant to take the bowl out of Harper's arms, but when the other woman turned with a thankful smile, it was the baby she handed her.

Stunned, Zoe held baby Lily at arm's length for a minute before pulling her in close. She closed her eyes for a second and breathed in the sweet baby smell of her before tickling her foot. "Hey there, cutie," Zoe cooed. "Are you helping Mommy?"

Beside her, Harper laughed. "I don't know about helping. But I came inside to grab some more supplies and this little missy had just woken up. Not that I expected her to have proper naps today. Not with so much going on. But still, one can hope." Harper laughed in that way that all new moms laughed when they were slightly overtired and overworked and their baby wouldn't sleep. "Can you hang on to her for a minute? I'll go grab a few more things and we can go down to the fire."

"Of course." Zoe nodded and shifted the baby into her other arm. Lily was almost five months old and at that super cute baby stage where she liked to giggle and smile at anyone who made funny faces at her. Something Zoe turned out to be very good at. For a few minutes, Zoe forgot about everything else, including the fact that less than an hour earlier, she'd made a huge, life-changing decision, and let herself enjoy Lily. The usual low-key sadness that seemed to swallow her up when she normally held a baby in her arms was lessened.

Maybe the doctors had been wrong? Maybe it would be different with a mate? Or maybe they would be perfectly happy without a baby of their own? Maybe—

"Thank you." Harper returned to the porch with a stack of paper plates and napkins. "She likes you." Harper gestured to her daughter with a nod of her head.

Zoe looked at the baby, who had reached for a hunk of her hair. She grabbed it and pulled so quickly, Zoe didn't have time to stop her. "Ouch." She moved to untangle her hair, but Lily had an iron grip. "You're pretty strong, kiddo."

"Here." Harper laughed. "Let me help. When she gets latched onto something, you would swear she has super-human strength." Harper put her things down and used both hands to unwind Zoe's hair, but before she released it, she pulled it back from her neck. "What the—Zoe?" Harper stared at her. "What is this?"

With her free hand, Zoe reached up and grabbed her hair, smoothing it back over her neck and the fresh bite mark Gabe had left there. "It's just a little—"

"Mating mark." It wasn't a question, so Zoe nodded, making Harper laugh. "What? Who? Gabe!"

It was Zoe's turn to laugh. "I thought everyone already knew," she said. "Chloe made it sound like the whole town already knew we were fated. You didn't?"

Harper shrugged and picked up her supplies again. "I was pretty sure. But I'm only half shifter, remember. I don't always pick up on things like the others." She turned before they walked down the steps together. "Of course, you don't have to be a shifter to see the heat between the two of you. And I did hear a little rumor about a game of pool that went unfinished at the Station the other day."

Zoe shrugged. Word definitely traveled fast around here. Not that it mattered. Not anymore.

"Well, I think it's great," Harper said as they made their way across the field. "Everyone loves Gabe. He and Ashton just fit in so well around here. I know everyone will be just as thrilled to see him happy and settled down again. It can't be easy to lose a mate and—I'm sorry, I shouldn't have said that."

"No," Zoe assured her. "It's fine. I know Gabe had a mate. I mean, Ashton's mom, right? And…I get it." She smiled, but she couldn't help but feel a flicker of discontent. *Did she get it?* After all, she didn't really know anything at all about Gabe's mate except that she'd died.

How had she died? What had it been like between them? Was it the same way with her? Had their connection been just as strong? Stronger?

All of a sudden, she had even more questions. Some of them didn't even make sense and made her feel like a jealous teenager.

"I'm sorry," Harper said again. "I didn't mean to say something to upset you."

Zoe shook her head. "You didn't," she lied. "Things are still so new. There's a lot I need to…well, all I mean is…" She looked up into her new friend's concerned face. "It's okay. Really."

It didn't matter that there was still so much she needed to know about Gabe and he about her. They had time. They had forever. All of her questions would be answered.

And hopefully, she would be okay with the answers.

"WELL, THAT DIDN'T TAKE LONG."

Gabe looked at his best friend. The flames of the fire provided enough light that he could see the teasing question in her eyes. He knew Bree had been dying to say something from the moment they got to the bonfire, but it wasn't until Ashton had gone off in search of a roasting stick and some marshmallows that she had her chance.

"I don't know what you're talking about."

She rolled her eyes. "So it's done?" she continued. "You're mated?"

Gabe didn't bother to hide his grin as he replayed their union in his mind. "She's mine."

"Wow." Bree shook her head and looked back to the flames.

"Wow what?" The smile fell from his face. "What does that mean? Weren't you *just* telling me not to fight it? You were literally just going on about how we were fated and everyone could see it and—"

"I still didn't think you were going to take her out into the woods like some *animal.*"

Gabe burst out laughing at her choice of words.

A moment later, Bree joined him as she realized how ridiculous she sounded. "Okay, never mind," she said. "But seriously." She touched his arm, making him look at her. "Does this mean you're not scared anymore?"

Belatedly, he remembered that he'd confided his fears in Bree. *Was he still scared?* The answer was more complicated than a simple yes or no and he was about to tell his friend that, when his senses alerted. He spun around and there she was.

Zoe.

His mate.

She walked next to Harper with baby Lily in her arms, and Gabe's bear rumbled within him. Before long, it would be *his* cub in Zoe's belly and in her arms.

Yes.

In a flash, everything became crystal-clear.

"No," he said over his shoulder to Bree, not taking his eyes off his mate. "I'm not scared of anything."

Chapter Ten

"DO YOU THINK WE'RE CRAZY?" Zoe nuzzled closer into Gabe's side and let the bedsheet slide off her. She didn't need anything but her mate to keep her warm. Besides, there was no way she could be cold after the hot lovemaking they'd just had.

As soon as they could, which was after Ashton had successfully made them each a s'more and had started falling asleep around the campfire, they'd snuck away from Grizzly Ridge and returned to Boulder Creek and Gabe's cozy house in town. Zoe felt a little bad that she hadn't said good-bye to Chloe, or told her where she was going, but at the same time, she was pretty sure it wouldn't take long for her to figure it out.

Ashton had given her a hug goodnight before Gabe carried him into his bedroom and tucked him in. Moments later, they were naked and in his bed, where they'd been ever since.

It was still dark outside, but Zoe knew it would soon be morning, and they'd be expected to get out of bed despite the fact that they hadn't actually managed to get any sleep. But between their lovemaking sessions and just talking, she wasn't in any hurry to close her eyes.

"No." Gabe answered her as he stroked a piece of hair

from her face and pulled her in closer to his chest. "We're fated. And there's a difference. A huge difference."

Zoe couldn't help but laugh. "I don't know. Right now, it sure feels like we're crazy. I mean, we barely know anything about each other. That feels pretty crazy."

"There's nothing I could possibly learn about you that would make me feel any different," he said seriously. "Nothing."

Zoe swallowed hard. *There might be one thing.* She'd done a good job pushing the concern about her fertility from her mind, but she wasn't stupid. She wouldn't be able to ignore it forever.

She snuggled closer and let a finger draw small circles on his chest.

"Can you tell me about her?" she asked after a moment. It was another thing she'd been avoiding. Not because she was jealous of the woman who came before her, but mostly because Zoe couldn't help but think it would be a sensitive subject. How could it not be? But she needn't have worried because Gabe didn't seem disturbed by the question. In fact, he didn't even seem surprised by it.

"Marie and I met when we were kids," he started without hesitation. "Our families were friends. We kind of grew up together, I guess. I remember thinking of her mom, Maryann, as my second mom for a while." He chuckled a little. "In fact, I think I actually loved her more than my own mom back then, too."

Zoe made a mental note to ask him about his parents later. For now, she just listened.

"It's funny because for the longest time, when I was young, I actually thought of Marie more as a little sister than anything else."

"Was it your families?" It wasn't unusual in bear clans for families to arrange the mates for their children in order to keep bloodlines strong, or to build alliances. And although her own parents hadn't ever pushed that on her or Chloe, they were black bears and she'd heard stories about how aggressive grizzlies could be about making matches for their children.

"No." Gabe shook his head beneath her. "It wasn't like that at all. Our families never pressured us to mate. If anything, it was the opposite. My mom and dad would talk about how Marie's family was cursed."

"Cursed?" Her finger stopped drawing circles momentarily. "What do you mean by cursed?"

"It was silly. At least, I thought it was." His voice lowered as he continued. "It was said that when a Grant mated, it would end in tragedy. Marie's dad died when she was only a young cub, and her grandmother too. She'd died long before Marie was born. In fact, if you looked hard enough, you could find a whole line of Grant grizzlies who'd died way too young. All were mated. With one cub."

"That's crazy!"

"Is it?" Gabe put his hand over hers. "Marie died. And if you ask my parents, it was all my fault."

Zoe slipped from his arm and propped herself up with an elbow so she could look into his eyes properly. She expected to see pain and hurt reflected in his dark eyes, but there was nothing there but affection and acceptance. "Why would it be your fault?"

"Because I mated her," he said simply. "If I hadn't have done that, she'd still be alive."

"She would have mated someone else."

"Maybe."

His simple answer prompted a new question. "Were you fated?" she asked before she could stop herself. "You and Marie? Was it like it was with us?" She braced herself for the answer, because for some reason she was worried that he'd say yes. *And so what if it had been the same? Would it lessen what Zoe had with Gabe?* She couldn't be sure but she had to know.

But she didn't have to give it any further thought because Gabe's answer came swift and sure. "Not. At. All." He sat up and grabbed her hands in his. "What you and I have...I've never experienced anything like it before." He looked straight into her eyes as he spoke and even in the dim light, Zoe could see the honesty and passion reflected in his gaze. "With you, it's..." He shook his head and took a deep breath. "It's like a magnetic pull I couldn't break if I was the strongest man on earth. From the moment I laid eyes on you, I—no." His lips twitched up into a grin. "From the moment I *scented* you, I had to have you. It was a primal urge and I knew that if I didn't make you mine, I would go crazy from the need."

As he spoke, her own need built within her like an electric charge that raced through her veins.

"With Marie, there was affection and love," he continued. "But nothing about our mating was instinctual or fated. Not at all."

"If it wasn't everything, then why mate?"

Gabe shrugged a little and nodded. "It seemed like the next thing for us to do. Like, the next logical step. I'd just finished my time at the police academy and she was almost done with college. She was going to be a teacher," he continued. "We cared about each other and...well...it just kind of happened one night."

Zoe nodded. She'd heard plenty of stories from her friends and cousins that sounded very similar. The concept of fated mates was more often than not considered a myth. Now she knew it wasn't. Far from it. But Gabe's story didn't surprise her.

"Neither of us even really thought about it," Gabe continued. "It was the same night Ashton was conceived and it just sort of happened. Now I wish it hadn't."

Zoe squeezed his hands. "Why? Why do you wish it hadn't happened?"

He looked down to their joined hands and after a moment when his eyes met hers again, they were full of sadness and regret. "Because," he said slowly. "I killed her."

GABE HAD NEVER SAID the words out loud before. Sure, he'd heard them plenty. Mostly from his own mother and father, who, upon learning they'd mated, yelled at him for enacting the curse that would surely be the end of Marie.

But Marie and Gabe hadn't believed in the curse. They'd laughed at it.

After all, how could mating and having a cub be anything but fantastic?

And it was. Their life together had been great. Gabe graduated from the police academy and got a job in their small town. Marie meant to finish school, but her pregnancy left her exhausted and she dropped out with only a semester to go. But motherhood agreed with her. Marie had blossomed into a fabulous mother and Ashton had been her entire life.

As time went on, the two of them would laugh at Gabe's still superstitious parents. "So much for a curse," they'd say. "Silly oldies."

But the Wilders still weren't laughing. They loved their new little grandson and relished the time they got to spend with him, but still they never tired of telling Gabe what a mistake he'd made and how he'd be sorry one day. Even when the young couple announced that they were pregnant once again, his parents weren't convinced that Gabe and Marie had snuck past the curse. "Only one cub will be born, and then the mated Grant grizzly will die," they said over and over.

It was morbid and annoying. Besides, Gabe and Marie

were untouchable. With every day that passed, they got more and more cocky and Gabe in particular even grew more reckless. He'd drive too fast, pushing the limits of their truck on the twisty mountain roads, but Marie would throw back her head and together they would laugh in the face of the destiny everyone was so sure they faced. She would be the first of the Grant clan to break the curse.

And then she'd died.

"I was driving too fast," Gabe recalled the story to Zoe. "I always drove too fast. And that day it wasn't raining, or snowing at all. In fact, it was a beautiful day with blue skies and..." He dropped his head as he remembered how they'd been on their way home from the doctor's appointment where they'd shown Ashton the ultrasound of his baby brother. It was going to be another boy.

He tried not to remember the image of the little *bean* that would have become his youngest son. They hadn't even had a chance to decide on a name for him before he was gone. If he let himself, Gabe would drive himself crazy wondering whether he would have been dark like his brother, or fairer, like his mother. Would he have been sensitive? A musician? Or rough and tumble like Ashton? There were so many questions that he'd never have answers for, and it brought him to tears every time he allowed his mind to go to those dark corners.

"Gabe," Zoe said tenderly, her voice thick with emotion. "You don't have to—"

"Yes." He looked up into her piercing green eyes and everything was okay. She was his. They were fated and it would be okay. There was no curse with her. They were meant to be and as terrible as he'd always feel about Marie, he knew she'd never wanted him to live his life with the curse weighing over him. Not when she was alive, and especially not when she was gone. "I need to tell you. It's okay," he said. "I'm okay.

"I lost control of the car," he continued the story. "And you know what the crazy thing is?" Zoe tilted her head. "I knew," Gabe said. "The moment the car started spinning, I knew it was the curse. And I know that she knew, too." He knew it wasn't rational and no matter how many times he remembered the accident and understood that it was impossible that in that split second, Marie would have had time to look at him and that they could possibly have exchanged a look that communicated what they'd probably always known and had only been trying to convince themselves otherwise, that the curse had finally caught up with them, he knew it was true.

"Gabe." Zoe scooted closer to him in the bed and put her hand on his leg. "You couldn't have—"

"No." He interrupted her softly. "We knew. It was the curse. She died because I mated her. I was reckless. I lost my mate and my unborn son. It was my fault," he said. "And my parents never let me forget it. So as soon as we could, Ashton and I moved here, to Boulder Creek. Marie's mom was already here and she's been a major help with Ashton."

They were silent for a moment as Zoe absorbed what he'd just told her. It only occurred to Gabe, belatedly, that he hadn't really answered her question. "I guess that doesn't really tell you much about her." He smiled. "She was a great person," he continued. "A fantastic mother and my best friend. She was my mate, but like I said before, as much as I cared about Marie, what we shared was nothing like what I share with you." He reached out for Zoe's chin and tilted it up so she was looking in his eyes. With any other woman, he would expect to see jealousy there, or hurt as she listened to him speak about another woman. But all he saw in his mate's eyes was love. "You and me, we're—"

"Fated." She kissed him then and climbed up on top of him until she straddled him. His hands came up to her hips and spread out over her smooth, bare skin. "I'm sorry," she whispered between kisses as she worked her way down his chest. "About what you went through and losing the baby, too. I can't even imagine that kind of pain." She stroked her hand down his cheek.

"I'm not going to lie to you and say it's been easy," he said. "Because it hasn't. I feel bad every day. Every single time I look at Ashton, I feel guilty. He'll never know his brother. Hell, he doesn't even remember knowing that he was going to be a big brother. He was so young when the accident happened. In a way, I think it was a blessing. I know it was a blessing." He dropped his head and shook it. "But at the same time…"

Zoe kissed him gently and looked into his eyes again. "Gabe, I think I should tell you—"

"No." He cut her off, because he was done talking about sad things or things that couldn't be changed. "No more talk about the past." He lifted her so she was directly above him, before flipping her over so he was on top of her. "It's time to look to the future. *Our* future. I believe everything happens the way it was meant to. I have Ashton and now I have you. Soon, I'll put a cub in your belly." He pressed a hand to her stomach and spanned his fingers over her soft skin. "*Our* baby. Ashton will know what it's like to be a big brother, and the curse will only be a distant memory. We can't change the past, it'll always be there, but now, we have the future."

It was his turn to kiss her then, a task he took to with enthusiasm. And when he bent to place a series of kisses on her stomach where hopefully soon their baby would be safely growing inside, Gabe was so consumed by love and passion for his woman that he completely missed the small sob that escaped her lips.

Chapter Eleven

THEY SHOULD HAVE BEEN EXHAUSTED after a night of no sleep, but by the time the sun slipped over the mountains and light began to filter through the curtains of Gabe's bedroom, Zoe was reenergized and ready for the day. In fact, she hadn't felt so light and full of energy in a long time. Maybe ever.

She rolled over to press a kiss to the tip of Gabe's nose. He'd only just fallen asleep, and although she would have loved to wake him if only to hear his voice again or feel the touch of his fingers on her skin because she knew she'd never be able to get enough of him, she also enjoyed watching him sleep.

Besides, it would be fun to surprise him with a full breakfast when he woke.

Pancakes or eggs?

She had no idea what he and Ashton would prefer. The night before, that might have concerned her, but between their lovemaking sessions, they'd talked and although it had only been one night, Zoe already knew so much more about Gabe.

The rest, she'd learn.

With one last look at her sleeping mate, Zoe slipped from the bed. She found one of Gabe's T-shirts and slipped it over her head. She'd never considered herself *petite* by any stretch, but his shirt fell nearly halfway down her thighs. It would be more than decent if Ashton woke up before she had a chance to change.

In the kitchen, she nosed around and found coffee filters and grounds. She set a pot to brewing before investigating in the fridge. She had her head stuffed deep inside when a little voice startled her.

"Dad keeps the cereal in the cupboard," Ashton said. "But the milk is in there."

Zoe stood back, the jug of milk in her hand. "I found it." She grinned. "But I was thinking…" She walked over to the boy and ruffled his hair with her free hand. "Maybe instead of cereal this morning, we could have pancakes? Or eggs?"

His eyes, miniature versions of his father's, grew wide. "No cereal?"

She shook her head cautiously and waited.

"Pancakes?" Ashton asked tentatively. "Or eggs?"

"Or both?" Zoe shrugged. "What's your favorite?"

"Both." Ashton jumped up and down. "Definitely both."

Zoe laughed. It was clear that for as great a father as Gabe obviously was, he likely wasn't the best cook. "How about you help me out?"

Ashton agreed readily and the two of them set to work preparing a big breakfast.

It didn't take long for them to fall into an easy rhythm. Ashton was a quick learner when it came to measuring and he was eager to learn. More importantly, he seemed excited for Zoe to be there. And not at all curious or confused as to why she would have slept over.

In any other circumstance, it would have felt strange to her, and she would never have spent the night. After all, there was a child involved. But it wasn't any other circumstance, and there was nothing *usual* about what was happening.

They weren't just any ordinary hook-up or relationship or whatever other descriptor you wanted to use. They were *mates*. And more than that, they were *fated mates*.

Which was why everything felt so absolutely *right*. As if they'd all been waiting their entire lives to wake up and make breakfast together. More than once, Zoe caught herself looking at Ashton in wonder as he stood guard over the rounds of batter she'd poured on the griddle. He had his spatula at the ready, waiting for Zoe to give the command that they were ready to flip.

"You're a pretty quick learner," she told him as she watched him flip the last of the pancakes. "Maybe you can teach your dad a few things."

With his spatula still in his hand, Ashton spun quickly on the chair he stood on and wrapped his arms around her. "Thank you, Zoe." He had a remarkably strong grip for someone his size—then again, he was a grizzly shifter—but it wasn't his hug that brought tears to Zoe's eyes. It was the sentiment behind it.

She had no idea how to handle such a situation. Or really anything about this situation. *Should she try to tell him about what was happening? That she was his dad's mate?*

But what about his mother? She'd been his mate, too.

Should she tell him that she was never going to replace his mother? *No. That wasn't right.*

There were so many questions, so many different ways to approach it.

In the end, Zoe did the only thing she knew how to do. She followed her heart.

She wrapped her own arms around the boy and hugged him back. "Thank *you*." She gave him a kiss on the top of his head. He smelled of campfire smoke, marshmallow, and little boy. Just like spending time with Gabe, being with Ashton just felt *right*. There was nothing more natural.

"I'm glad you're here," Ashton said when he unwound himself from Zoe's arms.

"You are?"

He nodded and turned back to his pancakes. "You make things brighter."

HE PROBABLY SHOULDN'T BE eavesdropping, but Gabe couldn't help it. When he'd woken to the delicious scent of coffee, followed by fresh pancakes, his stomach grumbled with need and he'd followed his nose to the kitchen. But the second he saw Zoe and Ashton together, all thoughts of breakfast and his empty stomach vanished as he watched his mate with his son.

His heart melted. Any last reservations he might have had about mating so quickly and moving so fast with Zoe vanished as he watched how easily the two of them worked together in the kitchen. Ashton was so accepting of Zoe's presence, and not only that, he really seemed to genuinely like her.

Was it possible that children felt the same natural pull toward mates the way that their parents did? And that Ashton was drawn toward Zoe because she was Gabe's mate?

He'd never had any experience with this type of situation before. Hell, he'd barely had any experience with mates, let alone second mates or *fated* mates. And none of it with a child before. He was completely in uncharted territory.

But by the looks of things, he had nothing to worry about.

As if Zoe and Ashton sensed his presence, they both turned around at the same time. Zoe's lips turned up into a slow, sexy smile while Ashton flashed him a toothy grin. "Dad! Look what we're doing. We're making breakfast."

"I love breakfast." Gabe crossed the floor and ruffled

Ashton's hair. "It's one of my three favorite meals. And it smells fantastic."

He moved over to Zoe, wrapped his arm around her waist, and kissed her chastely on the cheek. It felt as natural as if he'd been doing it his whole life. And he would be doing it for the rest of his life, too.

Not like Marie.

The thought crashed into him so unexpectedly, he took a step back.

"Is everything okay?" The smile fell off Zoe's face, replaced by a look of intense concern as she looked at him.

Gabe tried to force the thought out of his head, but yet it lingered. He'd thought the same thing with Marie. That they'd have forever.

But that was different. That was the curse.

It wasn't his fault; Gabe knew it. He really did. It had taken him some time, but he'd come to grips with the accident and the curse and the guilt that had left him devastated for months. Maryann had been a huge help for him while he'd worked through all those feelings, including the thought that his son might face the same fate as his mother. If the curse was real, Gabe couldn't bear to think about what would happen to Ashton one day. But he refused to believe it was real. It was the only way he could get through each day.

But he was in a better place now. He needed to remember that. With Zoe, it was different. *Everything* was different.

"I'm fine," he said after a minute. "More than fine, actually." The smile spread across his face and this time there was no dragging it off. "Really." He pulled her in and kissed her properly.

"Eww." Ashton laughed and jumped off his chair. "You can't kiss at breakfast."

"How about dinner, then?"

Ashton stopped gathering up the placemats and turned to stare at Zoe. "You'll be here for dinner, right?"

Gabe looked between them and waited.

Zoe crossed the floor and knelt in front of his son. "Do you want me to be here?"

He didn't hesitate. "Yes."

"Then I'll be here." Zoe wrapped her arms around Ashton and squeezed. "You're a very sweet little boy," she said. "Did you know that?"

Ashton nodded confidently and Gabe laughed. "My grandma tells me that all the time." He turned to grab the placemats and took them to the table. "She says I'm just like my mom was at my age. Did you know my mom?"

Just the way he always did when Ashton spoke about his mother, Gabe tensed a little. Because he was only two years old when she died, Ashton barely remembered his mother, which Gabe thought was both a blessing and terribly sad.

Zoe shook her head and helped him at the table. "I'm afraid I didn't know her, but your dad tells me she was a wonderful woman, and I believe that because you are an incredible kid."

Ashton nodded confidently before he turned to Zoe. "Are you going to be my mom?"

Zoe's mouth opened and shut and she looked at Gabe for help. As much as he was enjoying listening to their exchange, it was time for him to get involved. He couldn't even imagine how confusing the situation was for Ashton. Hell, it was confusing for him how fast he'd fallen for this woman. How did you explain that to a six-year-old?

He had to try though, so Gabe grabbed the plates from the counter and joined them at the table. "I know this is kind of crazy," he started. "Ash, you must be a little bit confused about why Zoe is here and that's my fault. I should have—"

"I'm not confused." Ashton sat up straight, looking much older than his young age. "When I met Zoe yesterday, I knew."

"You knew what?"

He shrugged. "That she was…" Ashton looked between the adults briefly before focusing on Gabe again. "That she was ours."

Chapter Twelve

THE DAYS ROLLED EASILY one into another and without any effort at all, the three of them settled into a happy family rhythm. Ashton's innocent words were exactly true: Zoe was theirs. And they were hers. Not since she was a small child had she felt so accepted and welcome in a family. She truly was home and it felt good.

But almost a week after the fall festival, despite how happy she was, Zoe had a niggling feeling of worry that had started to worm its way into all of her thoughts. As perfect as everything was with the three of them, she couldn't shake the feeling that it wouldn't last. That what was happening was only temporary and soon enough she'd be alone again.

Only this time for good.

The night before, Zoe had woken up with a start because her dreams had become a little too real. The room was dark. The alarm clock on the dresser said it was half past three. The sheets were twisted around her, and she was soaked in sweat. She'd taken a few deep breaths and let her breathing return to normal before she allowed herself to remember what she'd been dreaming about.

There'd been an accident. All three of them had been driving somewhere and then out of nowhere, a deer had run across the road, causing the truck to spin on the highway. And then the crash, the noise, and the screaming and…then she'd woken up.

It wasn't the first time she'd dreamed about an accident. That was the really alarming part. Every night that week, she'd had some sort of dream that involved an accident. They were always different. But also eerily similar. There was an intense feeling of loss, sadness, and death, but each time before she could see who was injured, she woke up.

What did it mean?

The night before, the dream had been even more real. More intense. She must have screamed out before she woke up because when her eyes snapped open, Gabe was there, rubbing her back and talking to her. He'd asked, but she refused to tell him about the dream. It was silly, she'd insisted; just a dream. Gabe had fallen back asleep, his arm around her holding her close. But even with his warm presence, it had taken Zoe another twenty minutes to fall back asleep. Thankfully, she didn't dream again.

Even after she showered and dressed for the day, with Gabe and Ashton already gone for school and work, Zoe couldn't shake the lingering effect of the night before. Somehow she needed to get to the bottom of whatever it was that was causing the nightmares. Maybe coffee with the ladies would help?

She'd really been looking forward to seeing Chloe and the others, and although she might not want to tell them about the nightmares, some girl time was probably exactly what she needed to clear her head and get rid of the bad dreams once and for all.

They'd arranged to meet up at Mountain Mama's for coffee and by the time Zoe walked in to the little cafe, half of the tiny tables were already taken up with laughing women. Zoe's face split into a warm smile as she was enveloped in hugs and greetings from these women she was very quickly coming to feel as family.

Was it really possible that she could be happy here like this?

Everything had happened so quickly and her feelings of wanting to run away from a life she thought she'd never be able to have had changed so completely, that mostly Zoe couldn't believe it was even happening to her. Everything she'd always wanted, was hers. Everything was perfect.

Except it's not.

Her smile dipped a little as that insistent and very annoying internal voice piped up.

"Zoe!" Chloe hugged her tight. "You look positively radiant." She turned to face the others. "Doesn't she look radiant?"

"Glowing."

"Almost as if—"

"Are you pregnant?"

The women all talked at once, and Zoe forced herself to keep the smile on her face because there it was, within a matter of seconds—the sharp reminder why everything was in fact *not* perfect after all.

"No." Zoe sat and hoped that would be the end of it.

"Well, soon then." Ella, who was pregnant with her and Kade's first cub, winked at her. "New love, am I right?"

Zoe shrugged, but Harper picked up the thread of the conversation. "I know it didn't take us long." She laughed and wiggled her nose against baby Lily's. "Axel and I couldn't keep our hands off each other."

"Us either." Kira rested her hands on her huge belly. She was only in her second trimester, but judging by the size of her, her twins were growing at an incredible rate. "I think it's the same for all of us, am I right?" She looked around and the women all laughed.

It was true. From what Zoe knew, they'd all gotten pregnant fairly quickly after mating with their partners. All but Chloe and Luke so far. She glanced at her sister, who smiled and mouthed the words, "Are you okay?" Chloe was sensitive to her situation, and Zoe knew she wouldn't tell the others if she didn't want her to.

"You'll be next, Nina." Bree pointed at Nina, who blushed.

"I never thought I even wanted children," Nina said. "What about you, Zoe?"

She almost choked on the water she'd just taken a sip of. *So much for a subject change.* She took a moment to compose herself before smiling as widely as she could.

"I have Ashton."

Bree beamed at her and pressed her hand to her upper arm. Zoe knew that Bree and Gabe were close friends, which just made the gesture that much sweeter.

"And Ashton loves you," Bree said. "He was so cute yesterday," she continued. "When I picked him up from school, he couldn't stop talking about you and how much he likes having you there." Just listening to Bree talk about Ashton made Zoe happy. "And I'm sure he'll be thrilled to have a baby brother or sister, one day, too. I know Gabe would love another child as well."

Hot tears pricked at the back of Zoe's eyes and she tried not to let her smile dip. "Maybe one day," was all she said.

Thankfully the conversation shifted away from children to other topics and soon Zoe found herself laughing and relaxing and not thinking about the huge secret she still hadn't discussed with Gabe.

"KNOCK-KNOCK." Gabe cracked open the front door and peeked his head inside. "Maryann? Are you home?"

It was a visit he'd been meaning to make all week, but on some level had been putting off. Sure, he'd seen his mother-in-law a handful of times throughout the week because despite the fact that Ashton loved Zoe and the two of them had taken to each other so easily, Gabe was cognizant that he shouldn't change too many things at once for Ashton. And he needed to make it clear to his son that just because Zoe was in their life now—and she most certainly was—it didn't mean that Maryann wouldn't still have a solid presence.

He also needed Maryann to know that.

"I'm out here," she called out.

Gabe followed her voice through the house and out to the back deck, where he found his mother-in-law stacking chairs.

"What are you doing?" He grabbed a patio chair and popped it on the top of the stack.

"Can't you feel it?" She held her head up to the air. "The chill is in the air. It'll snow soon."

Gabe shook his head. "It's too early." He knew better than to argue with his mother-in-law, especially when it came to things like the weather. She'd been living in the valley for a few years longer than he had, having moved right after Marie's death. "Too many sad memories on the coast," she'd said to him before packing up and leaving. "You're always welcome to join me."

He had and it was the best decision Gabe had made. Well, one of the best. Which was why it was so important that she understood that now that he had a new mate it didn't lessen his feelings for her or her role in his life. Not at all.

"Well, I'll trust you on this one." Gabe lifted another chair onto the stack. "But I sure hope you're wrong and we get a little bit more of this nice fall." Finished with the chairs, he moved to the patio table and started to pull the umbrella from its stand so he could secure it inside the garage. "Maybe if we're lucky, the nice clear days will hold out until after

Halloween." He chatted as he worked, and it took him a few moments to realize that Maryann wasn't joining in. He turned to see the older woman leaning against the side of the house, staring at him. "What's up?"

"I was going to ask you the same thing," she said with a wry smile. "Because I know you didn't come here just to talk about the weather and help me in the yard."

He chuckled. "Can't a man come by to say hi to his mother-in-law and help out with the yard jobs?"

"By all means." She crossed her arms. "You know you're always welcome here," Maryann continued. "But you also know you can talk to me about anything. Like that new mate of yours."

She added the second part so casually, Gabe was taken off guard and almost tripped over the bottom step of the deck. "What?"

"You heard me." Her smile was soft. "Come on inside and I'll make us a cup of tea so you can tell me everything you came here to tell me." She turned, but before she moved to go inside, she looked back at Gabe. "And just know, Gabe, I'm excited to hear all of it. It's about time you got yourself a new mate."

He didn't know what to say as he followed her inside. He hadn't known what to expect when he told Maryann about Zoe, but the one thing he did expect was that he'd be the one doing the telling. Now, it seemed that she would already know about it all. Then again, it was a small town and he shouldn't be surprised. But still.

"I'm sorry you didn't hear it from me first," he said when they were inside, around her oak kitchen table with mugs of steaming tea in front of them. "I should have come to talk to you right away when—"

"Stop." She held up her hand. "You can't possibly think that I would expect you to come running to your mother-in-law to tell her about your new love right when you're in the thick of it all, do you?" She chuckled. "Come on, Gabe. The last thing I expected was for you to think about me when you're with your new mate."

He couldn't help but laugh along with her. "Good point."

Maryann slid him the sugar bowl. "So, tell me about her."

Her smile was so kind, and even though Gabe knew it must hurt her on some level to have the discussion with him, she genuinely wanted to know, so Gabe started talking. Of course, he left out some of the more intimate details—they might be close, but they weren't *that* close—but otherwise, he told her everything he could about Zoe. When he was finished, she clasped her hands together and dipped her head.

"Maryann?" Gabe reached out and put a hand on her arm. "I didn't mean to hurt you or say anything that would—"

"You didn't." She shook her head. "I'm just so…" She blinked hard. "I'm happy for you, Gabe. This is what it's supposed to be like. The connection, hot and fast. Instant. You and Zoe, you're fated."

"That's what I think," he said. "Not that I really know, but it's just that it's so different…" He trailed off, unwilling to diminish what he had with Marie, especially not to her mother.

"It's okay," she said kindly. "I know how you feel because I know you and Marie loved each other fiercely, but you weren't fated mates."

"How did you know?"

"How did you know you and Zoe *were* fated?"

He paused and thought for a minute. "I just know."

"Exactly. Marie's father and I, we were fated. And as much as I love you, Gabe—and am thankful that you and Marie had each other—I've always known you two weren't fated, and that's okay. Not everyone gets to experience that kind of intense love, but it doesn't take away from what you two shared."

"No," he agreed with her. "It doesn't. I still miss her."

"Of course you do. But it's time you moved on. Past time. There's so much life left to live. There's no reason for you to be alone."

He nodded and let Maryann's words soak in. Neither of them spoke for a few minutes. They sat silently and sipped at their tea, each lost in their own thoughts and memories.

It was Maryann who spoke next. "I'm happy for you, Gabe." There were tears in her eyes as she spoke, but Gabe could see she meant what she said. "You deserve this. You and Ashton both. I can't wait to meet her. This woman who has stolen your heart so completely. She must be pretty remarkable."

He exhaled slowly. "She is." Gabe couldn't keep the smile off his face. "She really is. I think you're going to really like her."

"I think I will, too." Maryann stood and gathered up her empty tea mug. "Ashton has sure had a lot to say about her."

"Really?" Gabe assumed, but didn't really know whether he'd talked to his grandma about Zoe at all.

"Oh yes." She turned and smiled. "He told me that she just felt right."

Gabe laughed. "It's crazy, isn't it?" He swallowed back his question, again, not wanting to be insensitive. But he needn't have worried, because Maryann seemed to already know what he was going to ask.

"Crazy that Ashton likes her?" She shook her head. "Not at all. I haven't seen it very often, Gabe, where there's a child involved in a fated mate situation, but I think it makes perfect sense that Ashton feels drawn to Zoe as well. After all, the two of you are so close. He's bound to pick up on some of what's going on with you. And frankly, I think it just makes things that much better, don't you?"

He nodded and then, before he could overthink it, stood

and gave his mother-in-law a big hug. "Thank you, Maryann. Thank you so much."

She laughed, but Gabe knew tears were falling from her eyes. "Just be happy, Gabe. That's the best thing you can do for Ashton." She sniffed before she added, "And for Marie."

HE WAS GOING *to be hurt.*

Zoe revved the engine, pushing her bike to go faster as she flew down the mountain road.

He wanted cubs.

She squeezed her eyes shut as she rounded the bend in the road, opening them just in time to straighten the bike and accelerate on the straightaway.

Cubs.

Cubs she couldn't give him.

Zoe wanted to scream. Instead, she pushed the bike to go faster.

After her coffee with the ladies, she'd been unsettled and couldn't shake the conversation about babies and Gabe and how she was supposed to be next. *How could she tell her new friends that she wasn't able to have children?* She couldn't. Especially if she couldn't even tell the man she loved that she would never be able to give him more babies.

And she couldn't.

More than once over the last few days, she'd opened her mouth to tell him the truth, and then seconds before the words slipped from her mouth, it was as if she choked on them. She couldn't do it.

And she knew deep down that the reason she couldn't tell him was because it would kill him.

It might even be a deal breaker.

Could it be a deal breaker for fated mates? She didn't know enough about how it worked. But bonds between mates had been broken before. Surely, there were non-negotiables that were serious enough that they could fracture even the strongest of bonds between mates.

She didn't want to think about it. She couldn't.

So instead, she'd taken to her motorbike, pushing the machine harder and faster than she ever had before on the tight, twisty mountain roads. It was the only way she knew to forget about everything else. When your life was on the line, there was no room to think about anything else. Not even for a second.

Except the bike ride wasn't working. Not the way it usually did. Thoughts of Gabe and Ashton and the baby she'd never be able to add to their family kept creeping in.

If anything, the ride was only making things worse.

She had to tell him.

Now.

Without giving herself a chance to change her mind, Zoe turned the bike around and headed back into town and straight for the little bungalow she'd already started to think of as home. Gabe's truck had just pulled into the driveway, and Ashton was hopping out of the backseat as Zoe tore down the street and skidded to a dramatic stop in front of the house.

"That was so cool," Ashton hollered as soon as she pulled her helmet off her head. "Take me for a ride. Please?"

As soon as she saw Ashton, all her stress and worry evaporated, just the way it always did. With her helmet under her arm, she walked across the lawn toward them.

"Can I go for a ride, Zoe? Can I?"

"Sure you can!"

"Absolutely not!"

They spoke at the same time and it took Zoe a moment to realize that Gabe wasn't smiling the way she was. In fact, he sounded angry, and one look at his face confirmed it.

"What?" Ashton whined. "Why not, Dad?"

"Gabe, I don't see why he can't—"

"No." He cut her off. "You don't see." His mouth pressed into a thin line and his eyes were hard when he looked at her. "Do you know what we call motorbikes at the station?"

She shook her head, not because she didn't know what he was going to say, but more because she couldn't believe he was being so stubborn about it.

"Organ donors," Gabe continued. "We call them organ donors because that's what happens when you ride a bike. Accidents. Terrible accidents." He shook his head. "There is no way my son is getting on the back of that bike. Ever."

"What?" Ashton groaned and kicked a rock nearby. "That's so unfair." The boy turned and stormed off.

"Gabe." Zoe touched his arm. "It's really not that unsafe." She tried not to think about the way she'd just been riding. "And you know I would be extra careful with Ashton on the—"

"Zoe!" He spun around and grabbed her by the shoulders. "Don't you remember how his mother died? How could you think that I'd ever put Ashton in that kind of danger?" There was such intensity in his voice that it almost scared Zoe. "I can't expect you to understand," he continued. "I could never let anything happen to him, Zoe. He's all…"

His voice trailed off before he finished what he was about to say, but not before Zoe caught the meaning behind his words. "He's not all you have," she said gently. "You have me, Gabe." Tears sprang to her eyes. "And I would never let anything happen to Ashton."

"I know you wouldn't, not on purpose." Gabe used his thumb to gently wipe away a tear that had slipped from her eye. "You'll understand when you have your own child. It's like a little piece of your heart is out walking around in the world and even though you would do everything in your power to keep them safe, you know it might not always be enough."

She nodded as if she understood, but on the inside her heart broke. Because all at once, everything had become clear. Gabe was a father first, and fated or not, she'd never be able to give him what Marie had. She'd never be enough.

And it killed her.

Chapter Thirteen

IT WAS after midnight when Gabe was finally able to shut down his laptop and close up the house for the night. He seldom stayed up so late, and even more seldom was the reason for a late night due to work. And that definitely included staying up past midnight reviewing a case. But where Billy Benson was concerned, all bets were off.

It looked as if he'd been able to convince the appeal board to hear his case, which meant that Gabe had been called up to testify at the hearing. He'd do it without hesitation if it meant keeping the man behind bars, but he couldn't help but hate that the sleaze bag still had the power to make him crazy even all these years later. And he really hated that he'd taken out any frustration he'd felt toward Billy on Zoe earlier. And he had. He'd snapped at her and raised his voice when Ashton had asked to go for a ride on her bike.

He knew he'd overreacted. Just because he didn't want his son—or his mate, for that matter—anywhere near that motorbike hadn't given him any right to talk to her that way.

She'd insisted that she wasn't upset, but Gabe knew better. He knew something was bothering her. He could feel it. He also knew that he was the reason for those feelings in the first place. And he was definitely going to do something about it.

He opened the door to their bedroom and leaned against the doorjamb for a moment just so he could watch his beautiful mate sleeping. For the moment, her slumber was peaceful but Gabe knew that would change before the night was through. She seemed troubled by dreams and every night he would be woken by her thrashing in the sheets or calling out for something he couldn't quite understand. Some nights he was able to soothe her without waking her. He'd pull her into his chest and she'd snuggle close before drifting back into a hopefully dreamless sleep. But other nights, she woke herself. She was always embarrassed by her nightmares and tried to brush them off, so the last time it had happened, he'd pretended to be asleep.

He'd lain there while she sat on the side of the bed, waiting for her breath to slow. After a few minutes, she'd scrubbed her face with her hands and muttered something to herself before crawling back under the blankets to cuddle close to him.

Something troubled her, and Gabe knew without a doubt that if there was anything he could do to bring her peace, he would.

But the first thing he was going to do was apologize for his behavior earlier. Gabe shucked off his jeans and T-shirt and slipped under the sheets next to his mate.

Her body was warm and soft in all the right places, and when he pressed his own hard, muscular body up against her backside, she let out a groan in her sleep and instinctually snuggled back into him.

Just the feel of her against him made him hard but he wanted to wake her gently. Slowly. He wanted to be part of her dreams, and vanquish the nightmares once and for all.

Gabe forced himself to move slowly as he let one hand slip down the side of her bare thigh before he brought it up to her hip, slower this time. He continued the caress while he nuzzled into her neck and kissed her softly behind the ear. His lips traced his mark from where he'd taken her as his. He didn't need the light of day to know it was still red and contrasted sharply against her creamy skin.

She groaned in her sleep and wiggled instinctively against him so that Gabe had to hold back his own groan. She did things to him. Crazy things. Never had he felt so strongly about a woman before. Even now that they were mated, she still drove him crazy and made him want her with the slightest of looks. Zoe was incredible and Gabe knew he was the luckiest man in the world because how could he not be with such an amazing woman naked in his bed, reacting to him without even opening her eyes?

He slipped his hand up her smooth skin to caress her breast. He cupped it and squeezed, just enough so he could hear that sweet, sexy moan. Her breath came a little faster, her chest rising and falling with a little more urgency, but still she slept.

His cock was hard and hot between his legs, pressed up against her smooth skin, but Gabe would force himself to wait. As long as it took. He had a mission, and everything was about her.

Moving as slowly as he could manage, Gabe worked his hand down her body, gently skimming the sensitive skin on the gentle slope of her belly, until finally he reached the already wet cleft beneath.

His finger gently swirled in the wet heat between her legs and he had to bite back a moan. She was always so ready for him, so sweet and sexy and absolutely perfect. Her body responded naturally to his.

In her sleep, a sigh that spoke of satisfaction and...more... escaped her lips and Zoe spoke his name on a whisper as he snugged himself tightly to her.

So trusting. So giving. So his.

Before he could move again, Zoe, still sleeping, reached back between them, took him in her hand and squeezed.

Damn.

He kissed the back of her neck, and held her close with his hand splayed out over her belly as he slipped his cock between her legs and deep inside her.

SHE LET out a puff of air as he entered her. From behind her, Zoe heard him say her name on a moan.

She'd been having such a nice dream for a change. She was warm and safe and wrapped in a thick, knit blanket. Only it wasn't a blanket; it was Gabe. And with his arms around her, she felt safe and protected and…home.

In a state of half-sleep, Zoe realized on some level of consciousness that it *was* Gabe and she wasn't dreaming after all, that her life was just as amazing as a dream. She'd woken a little more when he snuggled closer, and Zoe knew instinctively what she needed from him, and was more than willing to take what she needed.

They moved together slowly and unhurriedly. They had all the time in the world, and he felt so good inside her, behind her, close to her. Zoe never wanted the feeling to end. She wanted him with her, this way, forever.

But soon the sensation intensified and her orgasm began to build deep inside her. She squeezed her eyes, wanting to escape inside herself and hold onto the feelings he created in her but at the same time ready to release them. Somewhere in her still half-sleeping state, she felt it start to crash through her. Behind her, Gabe tensed, and clutched her to him as they climaxed together.

When finally she'd caught her breath and opened her eyes

to become fully awake, Zoe let out a deep sigh of satisfaction and leaned her head back against her mate.

"Sleep well, my love," he whispered into her ear.

She smiled beneath his lips as he pressed a kiss to her cheek. "I will."

Gabe startled a little and pulled back, but not too much. "You're awake?"

"Barely," she admitted.

"I didn't want to wake you." There was the slightest pout in his voice. "I just wanted to give you something nice to dream about tonight."

"You did and I will." She turned her head to give him a kiss on the lips and a moment later was lying on her back, looking up into his eyes. "I tried to wait up for you," she said. "What time is it?"

He shook his head gently. "It's late. I'm sorry. I didn't mean to wake you up," he apologized again. "But now that you are…"

She giggled. "I don't think I have the energy to go again."

"That's not what I meant." He laughed. "Although, now that you mention it…" He blinked hard and his expression changed. "No, seriously, I wanted to apologize to you, Zoe."

"Apologize?" She blinked hard.

"I never should have gotten upset with you like that earlier." His voice was strained, as if it hurt him to speak. Not to apologize, but just to recount what had happened. "I'm worked up about something at work," he continued without prompting. "And then when I saw you, and I knew you were driving too fast and I just…well, I panicked. I can't lose you, Zoe." She sat up against the headboard and cupped his cheek with her hand. "I can't lose you," he said again. "And I can't lose Ashton. I just can't. And sometimes I think any idea of anything reckless… well, it scares me, Zoe. I know you're a little wild and I love that about you, but sometimes…I just want to tame that side of you to keep you safe."

"It's okay."

"No." He lifted her hand away and held it in his. "It's not. Because I never should have raised my voice with you. I know you don't get it. Not really."

His words were like a shot in her heart. *There it was again.* That she couldn't understand because she didn't have children. Which meant, she would never understand.

Because she couldn't have children. She'd *never* understand. She'd never get how he felt. And Gabe would never consider that her love for Ashton was enough.

Would it ever be enough?

Chapter Fourteen

ZOE BACKED SLOWLY out of the crawl space, dragging the big leather suitcase with her. "Are you sure this is it?" she called out to Ashton, who was waiting for her in the basement. He'd insisted that there was an old suitcase full of Halloween costumes in the crawl space. At least, he was "pretty sure there was." Either way, the kid needed a Halloween costume, what with the big day coming up quickly, and because he and Zoe were spending the afternoon together, it seemed like the perfect project to make sure he was ready to go.

"Is it a suitcase?" he called to her, his little voice muffled by the dark, damp space.

It seemed incredible that Gabe had so many boxes and things in the crawl space at all. After all, they hadn't lived in Boulder Creek for very long. Was it even possible to accumulate so many things in such a short time?

"It is," Zoe answered him. "Let's see what's in it." She pushed the suitcase out into the room.

It was layered in dust, but Ashton didn't care. He dove for the zipper and pulled it back, ready to discover what miraculous Halloween costume he was going to wear that year.

The cover dropped open with a small cloud of dust and Zoe barely held back a cough.

"What is this?" She didn't even have to look to know that the little boy was desperately disappointed with whatever he saw inside. "These aren't Halloween costumes!"

Zoe focused on what he was looking at. At first glance, Ashton was right. The garments that were in the suitcase didn't seem to be costumes at all. But when she lifted the brown shirt from the top and gently unfolded it, she could see that it was indeed a costume. It was a very old, drugstore-style cowboy costume made with material so thin, it almost disintegrated in her fingers.

"These are costumes," she told Ashton, because they were. The fact that they were at least thirty years old, and falling apart in her hands, and nowhere close to ninja warriors or superheroes that she knew Ashton was hoping for, didn't seem to be important.

Because either way, Zoe knew that Ashton was not going to be okay with the choice of costumes that they'd just pulled from the crawl space.

"Where's the ninja?"

Ashton stared longingly at the pile of worn fabric, and it almost broke Zoe's heart because she knew that there was no amount of searching in that old suitcase that would turn up the ninja costume he was so desperate for.

"I think we can do better." Zoe made a split-second decision and slammed the suitcase shut with another puff of dust. "You're going to have that ninja costume and you will be the toughest one in school."

"Not *tough*." Ashton moaned. "I'm going to be sneaky and…"

"Stealth?"

"Yes!" He jumped up and down, which Zoe was quickly coming to realize was his style. Ashton always did things at full tilt. "I'll be *stealth*." He spun around with his arms in a karate pose for a moment before his face fell. "But *how*, Zoe? How can I be a ninja?"

It didn't take her long to decide what to do. There was only one thing that *could* be done and Zoe was really hoping that the sliver of a plan she had would pan out the way she hoped it would. But all she could do was try. "I know exactly what to do." She jumped up from the floor. "Come on."

She led Ashton outside, stopping only long enough to grab their jackets and Zoe's motorbike helmet. "We need to go see Bree." Zoe handed Ashton an extra helmet without thinking it through. But when he didn't object, and slid it on his head, Zoe smiled. *He looked cute in a helmet.*

She was so focused on getting Ashton a costume, that she'd forgotten all about how Gabe had reacted to the motorbike only a few short days earlier. In fact, Zoe didn't think about the consequences of what she'd done while she was carefully navigating the bike down the streets of Boulder Creek, or when they were in the back rooms of Bree's Knees so Ashton could describe to Bree what he was looking for, or while she was measuring him, or even while they were climbing back on the bike to make the short ride home.

In fact, Zoe didn't give any thought to Gabe's objection to Ashton on the back of her motorbike one time. Not until she took a corner nice and easy, and her front tire hit a rock that had been kicked out into the asphalt by a large pickup truck that had sped through earlier. It wasn't until the motorbike started to swerve out of control and Ashton's little hands had clenched extra tight to her waist, his fingers digging into her flesh only moments before he'd started to scream, a sound that was only drowned out by her own scream as Zoe finally lost control of her custom painted Indian bike and it skidded along the pavement and she no longer felt his hands on her, that Zoe finally remembered how adamant Gabe had been at keeping his son off her *organ donor.*

———

"I'M sorry to be the one to tell you, Gabe." His captain from back home, Rex Williams, a man he'd looked up to and for so many years had helped Gabe get settled into the world of law enforcement, came across the line. "Billy Benson escaped from state prison last night. A manhunt has been mounted and we're increasing our—"

"He what?" Gabe cut him off. "You're what?" He shook his head and looked out over the mountain ridge. The moment the call had come in, Gabe knew he'd need to be parked when he took it, so he'd pulled his cruiser to the side of the highway before he answered. If Captain Williams was calling him personally, something had happened.

"I just got the word," Captain Williams continued. "Sometime last night. It was him and two other prisoners. They apprehended one, but Benson and one other are still on the loose. I thought you should know."

"Thank you." Gabe somehow managed to form the words but nothing made sense. "Wasn't the hearing scheduled for next week?"

"He was never going to win the appeal," Williams said simply. "And he knew it." Gabe could almost see the man nodding and chewing on a toothpick he long since should have thrown away. "So he ran."

"Shit."

"Shit is right, Wilder. You need to be on alert. We have reason to believe he's coming your way."

"My way?" Unable to sit still, Gabe undid his seat belt and stood on the side of the road. He needed fresh air, but no matter how deeply he breathed in, he couldn't seem to calm down. He didn't even need to ask why Benson was headed his way. But if there was new information, he needed to know. Now. "What do you know, Williams?" He probably shouldn't address his former superior in such a manner, but Gabe didn't care. He needed to know details, and he needed to know them quickly.

"There was a book found in his cell," Williams said. "It had your name scribbled in it. Repeatedly." His words made Gabe's stomach churn, but it was what Williams said next that made him almost throw up. "And through your name, every time, a line. He's coming after you, Wilder."

They spoke for a few more minutes, and Captain Williams assured him that he'd contacted his local captain and they were going to put measures into place to protect him, but Gabe knew it was all a bunch of talk. The only thing that was going to protect him and his family from that angry abusive piece of shit was going to be a shotgun.

"Fuck!" He yelled out into the valley and beyond as soon as he hung up the phone. The last thing Gabe needed to worry about right now was Billy Benson and his ridiculous revenge scenario that he'd spent the last few years building up in his head. He needed backup. And the only people he could think of to help him out were the Jacksons.

Gabe had no doubt that the Jackson clan would rally around him. He could take Zoe and Ashton up to the ridge and—

His thoughts and plans were cut off by his cell phone ringing and vibrating in his hand at the same time that a voice cracked over the radio.

"Gabe? Gabe, dispatch. Are you there?" He stared in disbelief for a moment. Dispatch never used his first name. They were never so cavalier about the way they used the radio.

"I'm here," he said after a moment. His phone still rang in his hand, but he didn't recognize the number right away. *Work first.* He needed to stay alert. "Go ahead, dispatch," he said into the radio.

"There's been an accident," Lois said. "You need to come to town."

"What?" Something was wrong. Lois didn't make callouts that way. "I'm fifteen out," he said into the radio. Surely there was someone else closer who could respond.

"Gabe?" Something in the dispatcher's voice stopped him. "It was a motorbike," she said. "Two passengers."

Gabe didn't hear anything else she said because a second later he was back in the driver's seat, his foot on the gas, two hands on the wheel, driving as fast as he could to the accident. And Zoe.

IT ALL HAPPENED SO QUICKLY that Zoe barely had time to process what was happening. But the moment she heard Ashton scream, the reality of what was going on slammed into her.

As soon as she moved, a sharp pain tore through her side. Probably a broken rib but she didn't have time to worry about it; she had to get to Ashton. Besides, she'd heal quickly. It wasn't important. Zoe pushed to her feet, ignoring the pain, and scanned the road for Ashton.

Thankfully, when the bike had gone into a skid, he'd fallen off into the grass on the side of the road and hadn't been pinned under the heavy machine. She spotted him next to a large pine. How he didn't hit it, she'd never know. Someone was definitely looking out for them. She shot a silent thank-you into the universe and sprinted over to the boy.

"Ashton. Where does it hurt?"

"Everywhere." His face was streaked with tears, but at least he wasn't screaming anymore. "Zoe?"

"I'm here. You're going to be fine." She kissed his cheek. "I promise."

That was the last thing that Zoe remembered before the first responders showed up and loaded them both into the ambulance. She refused treatment from the EMT, but there was no way she would leave Ashton's side. He didn't appear to have any major injuries, but his arm looked to be badly broken. He'd heal quickly. After all, he was a shifter. But children didn't heal as quickly as adults. That wouldn't happen until he went through puberty and shifted for the first time.

But it wasn't his physical injuries Zoe was worried about. It was the fear she saw in his eyes. Crashing on a motorbike was scary to be sure, but for a child who'd lost his mother in a car crash, it would be downright terrifying.

What had she been thinking?

Gabe was going to kill her. He'd specifically told her no motorbikes. He'd *told* her. And it didn't matter whether she thought he'd been overreacting at the time; Ashton was his son and—

"Zoe?"

She spun around and saw Gabe running through the doors of the emergency room. The doctors wouldn't let her back with Ashton because she wasn't his guardian. Instead, she'd been pacing just outside of the doors, driving the nurses crazy.

"Gabe."

He pulled her into a tight embrace and she winced as the pain from her rib shot through her.

"You're okay?" Gabe held her at arm's length and looked her up and down quickly. Satisfied with what he saw and with her nod that she was in fact, fine, he squeezed his eyes shut for a split second. "Thank God." He pulled her in for another tight squeeze. Vaguely, Zoe registered that Chloe and Luke had come in behind Gabe. Word got around in a small town. "I told you that bike was dangerous," Gabe continued. "We see too many accidents with motorbikes, Zoe. It's too dangerous. I don't know what I would have done if…wait, who was your passenger? Are they okay? What happened?"

It struck her that he didn't know that Ashton had been with her on the bike. But of course he wouldn't know. And he'd never expect it because, after all, it had only been a few days ago when he'd made it perfectly clear that Ashton was never to be on the back of her bike. He'd never expect her to disregard his wishes so nonchalantly the way she had.

Zoe squeezed her eyes shut and dropped her head.

"Zoe?" His voice was thick with concern. "What happened? Talk to me, Zoe."

"Gabe, it's…" She looked up and bit her bottom lip. "It's Ashton."

"Ashton?" He pulled away from her so quickly, she took a staggering step backward. "What about Ashton? He wasn't—"

"He was on the bike with me." The words started to flow out of her quickly because she knew she only had one chance to convey all the information that she needed to before Gabe would lose his temper. "He's going to be fine, it's only a broken arm and Gabe, I'm sorry, I really am, and it was just a short ride, I swear, and I was driving really carefully, we only went to Bree's to get a costume, and it wasn't supposed to—"

"He wasn't supposed to be on your bike, Zoe." His eyes flared and his jaw set. But the worst part was the way he looked at her. As though she'd done it on purpose. As if she could ever hurt Ashton on purpose.

But she had taken him for a motorbike ride when Gabe had made it perfectly clear never to do that. Did that mean that maybe she…*no*! She would die herself if anything ever happened to Ashton.

"Gabe, I…" She reached for him, but he turned away.

"Where is he?" He strode away, not waiting for an answer and leaving her standing alone as he went to the nurse's station and checked in. After a brief conversation with the nurse at the desk, Gabe disappeared through the door into the emergency room beyond and never even looked back.

She stared after him, and hardly noticed when Chloe put her hand on Zoe's shoulder. "Are you hurt? We heard about the accident." When she didn't answer, Chloe squeezed gently. "Zoe? Are you okay?"

Zoe shook her head, tears blurring her vision. "No," she answered softly. "I don't think I am."

Chapter Fifteen

"DAD, WHERE'S ZOE?"

Gabe looked straight ahead as he drove the cruiser down the streets of Boulder Creek, much slower than was necessary, but he wasn't taking any more chances with his son. It was at least the second time Ashton had asked him about Zoe since they'd checked out of the hospital. But it must have been at least the tenth time he'd asked that day.

And still, Gabe wouldn't answer him.

"Let's get you home, bud. You must be exhausted. It's been a big day." Gabe glanced in the rearview mirror and let his eyes rest for a moment on the bright-green cast on his son's arm. And just as it did every time he looked at it, the sight of his broken child squeezed his heart, causing a pain deep in his chest. He shook his head and looked away, focusing on the road ahead.

"I'm not tired, Dad." The whine in Ashton's voice said otherwise. "Where's Zoe? Is she okay?" His voice shook and sure enough, this time when Gabe looked in the mirror, tears were sliding down the boy's face. "I didn't see her again, and the bike was…and is she…"

"She's fine." Gabe softened his voice. Because as angry as he was with her, he loved her fiercely. "She's okay, buddy. She was just worried about you."

"Where is she?"

A flash of guilt shot through him. He'd been so consumed with worry for his son, and then so angry with her for putting Ashton at risk like that when he'd told her...he'd walked away from her.

Dammit.

Gabe swallowed hard. He'd just left her there. She was worried and terrified and had just been in a major accident and like an asshole, he'd turned away from her and—

"Dad!"

Gabe shook himself from his thoughts. "I don't know," he answered his son honestly. He didn't have time to say anymore because they'd just pulled up into the driveway of their house. The spot by the fence where Zoe had been parking her bike seemed strangely empty. Bile rose in his throat, knowing that bike had likely been towed to the salvage yard.

It could have been so much worse. I could have lost them.

Gabe helped Ashton out of the car and hovered as he walked up the steps into the house. He knew he was being overprotective, but he couldn't seem to stop himself.

Once he had his son settled on the couch with a movie he'd already seen a dozen times, and a bowl of ice cream in front of him, Gabe thought maybe that would be the end of the interrogation considering Ashton had something else to focus on, but he was wrong.

"Are you sure Zoe is okay?"

He wasn't sure. She seemed fine, physically. But emotionally, Gabe had no idea. If he had to guess, or listen to his bear —who knew much better than he did that Zoe was definitely *not* fine—he'd say no. She wasn't fine. "She's not hurt," he said after a moment. "But I think she was really worried about you."

"I'm okay." Ashton grinned, but the smile fell from his face as quickly as it came. "But I miss Zoe."

"She's not gone, buddy."

His words seemed to reassure Ashton and he turned his attention to the bowl of chocolate ice cream and the Transformers on the screen. But Gabe couldn't help but feel that he might have just lied to his son.

AFTER THE HOSPITAL, Zoe hadn't known where to go. Gabe didn't want her there, and the waiting room had started to fill up as word got around that there'd been an accident. Bree showed up with a woman that Zoe could only assume was Gabe's mother-in-law. Normally, she'd want to meet her, but things were anything but normal.

Things were only going to be awkward if she stayed, and harder than they needed to be, so after convincing Chloe and Luke that she was indeed fine, she left.

At first she didn't know where to go, so she just started walking. Pretty soon, her walking took her to the edge of town, where the trees that lined the sides of the road turned into thick forest. So she'd turned and started to walk directly into the forest until she was deep enough in the woods that she took her clothes off, carefully because her rib still hurt, folded them neatly and tucked them into a hollow log so she could find them later, and started to run.

Her body protested at first. The bruises, scrapes, and cuts from the crash ached and stung, but she ignored them and when she finally allowed her bear to take over, she screamed out in pain as her body shifted into her bear form. Her broken rib wasn't fully healed and she felt every bit of it, but she didn't care. If anything, she welcomed the pain. She deserved it. *She'd put Ashton in danger. She could have killed him. He was hurt and she'd walked away.* Pain was the very least she deserved.

Branches broke and crashed around her, but she barely felt them. All she could focus on was the breaking of her heart. Zoe pushed her animal through the trees, going faster and running harder until finally she collapsed in a small clearing. The sun had set and it had grown dark, the sky filling with stars while she'd been running.

She didn't know where she was, or how far she was from town, but it didn't matter.

Sadness overwhelmed her. She wanted to cry, to have some form of release for the pain in her heart, but the tears wouldn't come. Every time she closed her eyes, all she could see was Gabe's face and the anger when he looked at her.

She'd put his son at risk and it was clear that it was an unforgivable act.

Zoe couldn't begin to understand the bond between a parent and a child, but she loved Ashton. She was connected to him, too. Maybe it wasn't the same, but it killed her to think that her actions had put him at any kind of risk. Gabe must know that. He *must* understand that.

But what if he didn't?

She rolled to her back and stared at the stars overhead. How was it possible that only a few weeks ago she hadn't even known that Gabe existed and now...she didn't know how she was going to live without him?

GABE WAS SITTING up in the living room with all the lights off when Zoe came through the front door sometime after midnight and turned on the hall light.

"I wasn't sure you were going to come back."

She jumped a little at the sound of his voice but didn't seem too surprised that he was waiting.

He'd spent the last few hours wondering *whether* she would come back, or what he would say when she did, and that was the best he could come up with. He turned to look at her. "But I'm glad you did."

"How's Ashton?" She took a few tentative steps toward him and it broke Gabe's heart that there was a distance between them.

"He'll be fine." His lips twitched into a smile. "He's pretty excited to show his friends his cast. It's green."

"Of course it is." She gestured with her head to the spot next to him. "Can I sit?"

Gabe nodded, but instead of waiting for her to sit next to him, he reached up, took her hands and pulled her down to his lap. Her legs straddled his so she faced him. She didn't resist but he could feel that something had changed between them. He knew he'd been harsh with her; he knew he'd screwed up. But he also knew that what she'd done wasn't okay.

"Zoe, I…" His hands floated down her sides before finally coming to rest on her hips. "I'm just so…God, I'm so thankful you're okay. You *are* okay, aren't you?"

She nodded. "I'll be fine."

"You could have been killed." The anger and fear and emotion from earlier rose up within him once again. "Ashton could have been…" He dropped his head and shook it before looking up. "I don't know how I can be so angry with you and so happy to see you okay at the same time. I don't know how to…dammit, Zoe, I don't know how to do this."

"Shh." She grabbed his face in her hands and held it so he had no choice but to look her in the eyes.

In that instant, looking at his mate, everything else was forgotten. It was only the two of them and they were together and everything would be okay. Zoe kissed him softly. Her lips pressed against his and something inside him snapped. She moved slowly and didn't release her hold on his face while their tongues found each other.

The taste of her was almost enough to make him break altogether. Too many emotions. Loving her was intense in a way that Gabe wasn't really sure how to deal with. His hands slipped under her T-shirt so they could feel her bare skin. She gasped a little when his touch skimmed over her side.

"I need you, Gabe," Zoe whispered in his ear as he lifted her shirt off and over her head. "I need to feel you." There was a desperation in her voice that made him think she was on the verge of tears, but his own need for his mate was so great, it must have been the tangle of emotions they were both feeling.

As gently as he could, Gabe lifted her and carried her into the bedroom. He put her down on the bed and pulled her jeans off before shucking his own to the floor and pulling her on to his lap. The moment she was in his arms again, Gabe's lips crushed to hers with a renewed ferocity.

Zoe's hands slipped under his shirt and lifted it over his head so they were both naked, hot skin pressed together. His desire was hard and hot beneath her, and with her mouth on his, Gabe lifted her gently and brought her down slowly onto him so his hard length filled her.

She gasped and tucked her head into his neck.

Gabe stilled, giving her a moment to grow accustomed to him, but it was Zoe who started moving. She set a slow rhythm with her body, and her mouth found the still tender mark she'd left on his shoulder. Her tongue traced the mark, and Gabe thought he'd come undone right then.

It didn't take long before he felt her start to shake, just a little, against him and he knew her release was close. Zoe kept her mouth on his mark and he held her close to him while her orgasm, strong, silent, and with an intensity that Gabe felt right to his own core, rolled through her, moments before his own climax ripped through him.

Neither of them moved for a moment, the intensity of what they'd just shared silencing them. It wasn't until after Zoe sat back that Gabe realized she'd been crying.

Chapter Sixteen

ZOE HAD NEEDED him one more time because something had shifted between them and she knew there was a chance that it might not ever be the same. She knew it was selfish, but she'd needed to feel him close again, so she could remember the moment.

"Babe? What's wrong?" Gabe reached out and used his thumb to wipe a tear from her cheek. "It's okay. I—"

"No."

She saw his face change and Zoe knew that Gabe, too, was thinking of the scene at the hospital. The way he'd looked at her. The anger in his eyes. The disappointment.

"You need to believe that I'd never do anything to hurt Ashton," she said slowly. "It was an accident and I know that I never should have had him on the bike. It was a mistake."

"Mistakes can—"

"No." She shook her head to quiet him. "I know. I screwed up, Gabe. I know. You need to know—no, you need to *believe* that I'd never do anything to hurt Ashton. I love him like he's mine." She looked down for a moment and chuckled a little when she lifted her head again. "I know it's crazy, but it's the same with us, Gabe. I feel it. Ashton is mine and—"

"No." He cupped her face with his hand. "He's not. Not like that. Not in the way that you feel a physical pain when something happens to him. Not in the way that you watched him take his first breath, his first step, you heard his first word." He shook his head and a searing pain stabbed Zoe in the heart. "You can't understand, Zoe. Not the way I do. When you have your own—"

"No." She stood up off his lap and when he reached up to pull her back down, she pushed him away. "You're wrong." Every word caused her physical pain, but it needed to be said. "I won't ever know." Her words came out as a choke. Maybe it needed to be said, but it was going to be hard as hell to get the words out. Zoe turned away, but could feel the heat of Gabe's body as he stood up behind her. He wasn't quite touching her, a detail she was glad of because she didn't think she'd be able to manage it if he did. She had to tell him the truth, that she'd never be enough for him, and if he touched her, she might lose what little resolve she had left.

"Zoe, I wasn't trying to say that you don't care about Ashton or love him, but—"

"You were just saying that it's not the same thing." She turned and crossed her arms over her bare chest, feeling much more exposed than she would have liked. "I get that I can't possibly understand what it's like to feel that connection with a child who isn't mine."

"But you'll get it." He reached out for her, but she shook her head and took a step back. She couldn't look him in the eyes. Not yet. "Wait until you have—"

"I'll never have a baby of my own." The words fell from her mouth. "I'll never know what you're talking about, Gabe. I can't."

"What are you talking about?" Again, he tried to take a

step toward her, but Zoe stopped him with a shake of her head. "We'll have a—"

"I can't have children, Gabe. I found out officially a few months ago." Her voice cracked, but she managed to hold it together. She didn't have any other option. She had to. "I know I should have told you before."

"Wait. What?"

Finally, she met his eyes and when she did, she wished she hadn't. There was confusion and hurt there when just a few minutes earlier, there was love and adoration. The change killed her.

"I know I never should have kept it a secret."

"Zoe?"

"It was just that when we met, we had such an amazing connection."

"Wait, Zoe."

"And now we're mated and I can't give you what you want. I just—"

"Zoe!" He grabbed her arms and shook her just enough so she'd look into his eyes. "Just stop."

Tears streamed down her face now and looking at him broke her heart because she knew without a doubt that he was about to do what she should have done from the very beginning. Just like every other bear shifter, she knew Gabe needed a mate who could give him more cubs. Especially after the loss he'd endured. Gabe not only needed that from her: he *deserved* it. Ashton should have siblings. The bloodline should be continued.

She'd made a mistake. She'd allowed herself to fall for him, to mate with him, and worse, to lie to him. But the truth was, she'd never be able to be what he needed, and he'd resent it. Worse, he'd never be able to feel about her the way he felt about Marie. She'd given him a son. And all she could give him were lies.

"No." She shook her head. There was no doubt about what Gabe was going to say. But she wouldn't let him. She loved him too much to make him say it out loud. "I can't," she said. "I can't stop because I know what I've done is terrible and I'm so sorry. I'll release you. You can mate someone else. You can have the family you deserve." She moved quickly then and pulled from his arms to retrieve her clothes.

Now that the words were out of her mouth, she couldn't take them back and she couldn't stay in the same room as him. It hurt too much.

"Zoe, don't do this."

She didn't turn around. She tugged her jeans on and pulled her shirt over her head.

"Zoe!"

She turned then, more because she needed to see his face one more time than because anything he could say to her would help her change her mind. She knew it wouldn't. There was no other choice. The moment her eyes locked with his, a sob escaped her throat.

GABE COULDN'T WRAP his head around what was happening. The sudden shift in Zoe was confusing, but maybe not as perplexing as he'd first thought. Had his coldness at the hospital, his anger toward her, had it really caused this?

No.

She couldn't have children. She'd lied to him.

No.

She hadn't lied. But she hadn't told him.

But it wasn't a deal breaker. *Was it?*

Gabe thought of Ashton. That boy was his entire world. No. He *had* been his entire world. But that world had expanded when Zoe came along. She was his mate. He loved her. He *needed* her. Surely, she felt the same.

Nothing made sense and she wouldn't stop talking long enough for him to sort it out.

When she finally turned around and he saw the tears in her eyes, the pain written all over her face, it almost broke him. Gabe took two steps until he was right in front of her and gripped her arms. "Tell me what's going on here," he pleaded with her. "I don't understand what's happening. You're not leaving."

"I have to."

"No." His voice was firm, bordering on panic. "You don't. I need you here."

"You don't understand."

"I do." He wasn't sure he did. Not at all. But that didn't seem important. The only thing that mattered was keeping her there with him. Because if she walked out the door, he wasn't sure he'd know how to carry on. "I understand that your mine and I'm yours and we can figure out everything else."

Her smile was soft and so sad it hurt his heart. "Gabe, I'll never be able to give you cubs."

He shook his head. "That's not—"

"It is important and we both know it. It's in our blood."

That didn't make any sense. She was a black bear. He was a grizzly. Any children they had weren't going to be pure anyway. Even if he did care about that kind of thing, it wouldn't matter. He told her so, but still she shook her head.

"I realized something today," she said. "The way you felt about Marie, that will always be—"

"Don't compare this to what I had with Marie." He stopped her. "It's not the same."

"No. Because I can never give you a child." Tears streamed down her face and he yearned to wipe them away, as if it were that easy to fix what was going on between them. "And today when I saw the way you were with Ashton. And when you said that I couldn't understand—"

"I was wrong." He shook his head. "I said those things because I was upset. I was worried. I didn't mean them."

"Yes, you did. And that's okay." Again, she tried to smile through her tears. "Because you were right, Gabe. I can't be what you need. I can never give you what you need and as much as I love Ashton, and I do—" She choked on a sob before continuing. "You're right. I'll never know."

He stared at her for a minute, willing her to come to her senses and to believe what he said. He needed her to recognize that it was just an accident and he'd only said those things in the heat of the moment.

Hadn't he?

Had there been some part of him that really did believe that? That believed that she could never love Ashton the way he did? The way his mother had?

Maybe.

"Is this what you really want?" he asked after a moment. He dreaded the answer because he already knew what it was and a part of him died when she finally nodded.

"I wish more than anything it could be different," she whispered. "But I love you too much for you not to have everything you need. More children, a brother or sister for Ashton. Someone who understands the type of love I never can." She leaned forward and kissed him softly on the lips. Before he could react to what had happened, she was gone.

For the second time in his life, Gabe's world shattered like glass around him. In an instant, everything had changed and for the life of him, he didn't know how to put these pieces back together again.

Chapter Seventeen

FOR THE NEXT FEW DAYS, Zoe split her time between the couch in the Den at Grizzly Ridge where she would curl up in a fluffy blanket and stare into the fire the Jackson brothers kept roaring in the hearth, or on the trails that wound through the woods, taking her to various gorgeous ponds, waterfalls, stunning vistas and views out over the valley and a variety of other spectacular sights that barely registered in her brain.

The only thing that did register was the overwhelming weight of sadness that hung over her. Chloe told her she needed to sleep and that she'd feel better if she got a little rest, but she couldn't close her eyes because every time she did, she'd see the look on Gabe's face right before she'd turned and left him. And when she did manage to push through and fall asleep, she'd dream of the accident, of Ashton's scream. Of his little body lying helplessly on the asphalt. Only in her dreams, it wasn't just a broken arm.

She couldn't bear it. Any of it. It hurt too much.

"Zoe?"

She heard Kira's voice, but couldn't manage to even acknowledge the other woman. A moment later, she felt the shift of the couch cushions as Kira lowered her and her ever-expanding belly to the couch next to her.

"Zoe?" Kira's voice was soft, the touch of her hand on Zoe's arm even softer. "I know you probably don't want to talk right now."

Zoe shook her head, but Kira kept talking.

"And probably especially not to a pregnant woman, right?"

She had that right.

Zoe shrugged and kept looking at the fire but Kira was not deterred.

"I know you're hurting." Kira squeezed Zoe's arm. "And I wanted to talk to you because while I don't know what you're going through, I know what it's like to feel like you need to make a choice when it comes to love. But you don't."

Zoe squeezed her eyes shut. She didn't know all the details about Kira's situation but what she did know was that a few years earlier, she'd mistaken a bad situation for her fated mate and had left her brothers and her clan for years. While she'd been gone, she'd fallen in love with Nash, a wolf, and also her fated mate. It was definitely a complicated situation, but now Kira was back, with her mate, and was pregnant with twins. Yes, definitely complicated. But they were making it work. And they were thriving.

Maybe it was possible?

No. She couldn't let thoughts like that seep in. It was different with her and Gabe. So different.

After a moment, Zoe lifted her head and looked at her new friend.

"But what if I make the wrong choice?"

"Do you really think it's only your choice to make?" Her smile was kind, but Zoe couldn't help but feel as if she'd been slapped in the face.

"I know he'll choose me," she said after a moment. That wasn't the problem. The problem was what if Gabe chose her and then changed his mind when he realized that what he thought wasn't important actually was? She told Kira as much. "I don't think I could survive that."

"Yes." Kira squeezed her arm. "You could. And it won't matter because that would never happen. You two are fated."

Tears slipped down her cheeks. "But even fated mates aren't as strong of a bond as father and child and…"

"Zoe? It doesn't have to be a choice. You know that, right?"

She shook her head.

"The bonds between mates and cubs are different. It isn't one or the other."

Logically, of course, Zoe knew Kira was right. But she hadn't seen the look on Gabe's face when Zoe's actions had put Ashton in the hospital. It was clear, crystal-clear, that there was one bond Zoe couldn't come close to.

She didn't say anything else, but simply shook her head and looked back into the fire and together they sat in silence until finally Kira wrapped her arm around her shoulders and squeezed. "We're here for you no matter what you decide."

"Thank you."

"He keeps calling, you know?"

Zoe nodded. She knew. She'd turned her phone off, but she knew that Gabe had been calling the ridge and Chloe, too. She'd seen his truck in the yard at least twice, too.

"He loves you."

Zoe closed her eyes.

"What about Ashton?" It wasn't Kira's voice that had asked the question; it was Chloe's. Her sister hadn't said much when Zoe came back to the ridge to hide out and Zoe knew it was because Chloe thought she'd made a mistake.

"Sorry, Kira," Chloe said. "I didn't mean to interrupt, but I think there are a few things my little sister needs to hear."

Zoe shook her head, still unwilling to open her eyes. "Chloe…"

"No, Zoe. I need to say this and you need to hear it. Whether you look at me or not, I'm saying what I need to say." She didn't wait for a response. "You're being ridiculous. Gabe loves you and you love him," she started. "You're fated, for bloody sake. That doesn't go away. And it certainly doesn't change just because you can't have children." Her eyes snapped open then and she glared at her sister but Chloe continued. "You were wrong not to tell Gabe, yes. But do you really think that would have changed the connection between the two of you? Do you think that would have made anything different? Honestly."

Her instinct was to nod, but she knew that wasn't true. "No," Zoe said softly. "It wouldn't have changed anything."

"So why now? What has changed now? He still loves you. He's still your mate. So what—you can't have children. That doesn't change anything between the two of you. And more so, it doesn't change anything with Ashton. Have you even thought about that poor boy?"

She had. A lot and it broke her heart.

"He's already lost one mother and just when he found you, you decided to leave. With no explanation. Nothing. He's a child, Zoe. And more so, he's your fated son."

Chloe's words crashed through her.

"My what?"

"Your fated son."

Next to her, Kira squeezed her arm again, grounding her to the moment. A gesture she was thankful for.

"My fated son?"

"Think about it, Zoe," Chloe continued. Her voice was firm, with the no-nonsense tone she'd always used when they were kids and she was trying to boss Zoe around. "Just think about it. Some things are about more than you think they are."

IT WAS GOING to be one of those nights. Halloween always was. Even in the sleepiest of towns, Halloween always seemed to bring out the crazy side of people. Normally, Gabe didn't mind the challenge of a busy night, but for the last few days since Zoe had left him feeling confused, heartbroken—and a little pissed off, if he was honest—the only crazy person he wanted to deal with was her. And crazy was the only way to describe the way she was acting right now.

She wouldn't answer his texts or calls. And she refused to see him the few times he drove out to Grizzly Ridge. He didn't know what else to do and was about to enlist the help of some of the Jackson brothers when, just the day before, he'd received a text from her saying that she would still like to take Ashton trick-or-treating the way they'd planned.

The plan was for Zoe to pick Ashton up from Maryann's, take him home to change and then out to trick-or-treat.

Maryann was more than happy to let Zoe take over again and with Gabe having to work, there was no reason for Gabe to say no. Besides that, Ashton hadn't stopped asking about Zoe and when she was coming back. It broke his heart to see his son so confused about what was going on, especially considering he didn't even know what to say to make it better for him or to explain it. *How could he when he didn't know himself?*

He shook his head and reached for his coffee.

"Hey, Wilder." Gabe spun on his stool where he was working through his second cup of Alyssa's famously thick, dark coffee at Mountain Mama's. They were using the cafe as a staging area for the volunteer patrollers who were helping out on the busy night.

Kade Jackson and Brian Blackwood stood in the door, their large frames blocking it completely.

"Hey, guys." Gabe lifted his hand in a wave. "You guys are early for patrol." The men had volunteered to help out with citizen patrol. Halloween was always the busiest night, and

Gabe knew that having the big shifters walking the streets of Boulder Creek would be a huge help to prevent mischief, and he'd take all the help he could get.

"Looks like you had the same idea we did," Brian said. "A little of Alyssa's rocket fuel to get us through the night."

The woman behind the counter snapped her gum and put a hand on her hip. "You can't fool me, Brian. I know you wake up craving my coffee."

"Not as much as I crave you, Alyssa."

She rolled her eyes, but Gabe didn't miss the blush that crept up the young woman's face as she poured the new arrivals each a coffee. Alyssa and Brian had been flirting for years since Alyssa and her brother had moved to town only a year before Gabe had. They both denied it, but anyone could see they had a connection. It was a mystery to Gabe why they didn't just get it over with and hook up. But he wasn't about to pretend that he understood wolf shifter relationships. Hell, he couldn't even understand his own.

Brian followed Alyssa to the other end of the counter, no doubt to continue his shameless flirting.

Kade just shook his head and pulled up the stool next to Gabe. "How are you hanging in there?"

Gabe didn't bother asking his friend what he was talking about. There was no way that his relationship problems were a secret. Not in this town. "Not good." He lifted his cup to his lips. "Women."

Kade laughed. "I get it. I do. And I wish I had some advice for you, man. But…"

"Do you think that the bond between a father and child is stronger than the one between mates?" Gabe hadn't planned to ask the question. Hell, he hadn't planned to talk with Kade about his troubles at all, especially not right then. But as soon as his friend sat down next to him, the urge to talk was strong.

Besides, maybe the man could offer some kind of insight. He'd take anything.

Kade wasn't fazed by the question. Instead, he sat back and took a breath. "No," he said after a minute. "I don't think it's stronger. I think it's different."

Gabe nodded, but didn't say anything. All week, he'd been replaying Zoe's words in his head. He knew he'd overreacted when Ashton broke his arm, but...had she been right? *Would he ever be able to love her the way he loved his son? Would Ashton always come first? Shouldn't he? What if Zoe couldn't give him any children? Did that matter?*

So many questions.

"Keep in mind," Kade was still talking, "my cub isn't even born yet, but I already feel a possessiveness and protectiveness over him that I've never felt before. And I've definitely felt both of those things for Ella. But it's different. Not stronger. Not better. Just different."

"Different," Gabe repeated. "And that's okay."

"Hell yes," Kade said. "That's more than okay. That's the way it is and should be." He turned on his stool so he faced Gabe. "Tell me one thing, Wilder. Can you live without her?"

He didn't even have to think about it, but before he could answer, his cell phone rang. A number that had become all too familiar in the last few weeks lit up the screen and his stomach clenched, his instincts kicking in.

Captain Williams.

With the craziness of the last few days, he'd forgotten all about Billy Benson.

Shit.

He didn't have to answer the call to know it wasn't good news.

DRESSED IN HER PIRATE COSTUME, Zoe should have felt ridiculous driving through town in the truck she borrowed from Luke. She felt anything but. Chloe's words a few days earlier had hit home, and although she still had a lot more thinking and processing to do, there was one thing she didn't need to think about any more.

How she felt about Ashton.

And Chloe was right, at least about some things. She cared about him. A lot. And it wasn't fair that she'd just disappeared without any explanation. He deserved at least that. But first, he deserved the trick-or-treat experience she'd promised him when they'd gone to Bree's to get fitted for Halloween costumes. And that's exactly what she was going to do.

Bree had talked them into costumes that were entirely different from the ninja that Ashton had his heart set on and when she'd suggested pirates, Ashton had jumped on it. Bree had outdone herself and even though Zoe hadn't seen Ashton's costume yet, hers was amazing. Bree really was talented at what she did.

She arrived at Maryann's house and Ashton ran out the door as if he'd been watching for her. His little boy body slammed into her legs and he wrapped her up in a hug.

"Are you excited, buddy?" She had to fight back tears. *How could she have walked away from this kid?* No matter what happened with Gabe, she knew Chloe was right: her connection with Ashton was fated.

So is your connection with Gabe.

The little voice in her head was growing increasingly insistent and Zoe was about ready to tell her bear in no uncertain terms to shut the hell up.

"Can we go right away, Zoe?" Ashton was chattering on about the streets he wanted to trick-or-treat on, and what houses had the best candy and where the haunted houses were set up.

It was all Zoe could do to keep up. She nodded and laughed and answered him the best she could before she looked up to see Maryann watching them.

"Hi." She lifted her hand in a wave. "I'm Zoe. I guess we haven't met yet." She thought that meeting Gabe's mother-in-law might be awkward, but the other woman smiled warmly.

"I'm very happy to finally meet you, but I wish that—"

"It's going to be a fun night." Zoe cut her off before she could say anything more. She didn't know how much Maryann knew, and it wasn't the right time to find out. "Thank you for letting me take him out tonight," she said to the older woman. "I know that…well…I mean…thank you," she finished lamely.

Maryann waved her hand. "It's nothing. To be honest, I'd rather stay home and see all the kids dressed up and I know Ashton would rather go with you."

"Grandma, I didn't—"

"Hush." She laughed. "And get going. You still need to get your costume on. You don't want to waste a minute."

"She has a point," Zoe said to the boy, but Ashton didn't need to be told twice. He was already on the way to the truck. She took one last look at Maryann, who was watching her with a soft smile, waved and took off for Gabe's house.

In and out. That was the plan. They were only going to stop at the house long enough for Ashton to change and grab a trick-or-treat sack, and then they'd hit the streets.

When she pulled up in front of the little bungalow she'd grown to call home, even if it was for a short time, Zoe's heart tightened in her chest.

This should be your home.

She shook her head. She *would* quiet her bear. She had to. It didn't know what the hell it was talking about.

Zoe still had a key, so she unlocked the front door while Ashton bounced up and down next to her.

"Okay, go change," she told him. "I'll go find some bags to use for candy collection. Meet me back in five minutes."

Zoe laughed as he took off without a word. No doubt he'd be back in two minutes. She'd never seen a kid so amped up. She hurried into the kitchen to find some bags to use as trick-or-treat sacks but the moment she entered the almost dark room, she knew something was wrong.

Her bear roared and her instincts kicked into overdrive.

Zoe scanned the room and at the same time took a step back. Straight into the hard wall of a man.

In a second, the stranger's arms were around her and covering her mouth.

She thrashed against him, but his arms were like steel vises holding her in place. She tried to scream and bite at the hand, but he only pressed it tighter to her mouth, squeezing the sides of her face.

"Shut up," he hissed in her ear. "Not one word or I'll kill you."

She believed it. He had the sound of a desperate man and with Ashton in the house, it was not a bluff she was willing to call.

Without warning, the man spun her around and shoved her into the corner so she crashed hard against the cupboard. Somehow she managed to stay on her feet, but she moved backward so she was pressed up against the cupboards as far away as she could get and assessed her assailant for the first time.

He was a shifter. But not a bear. Or a wolf. A cat of some kind. She couldn't think. He was dirty and even from a distance, his rank scent filled her nostrils.

"Who are you?"

He took a step toward her, his lips curling up in a sneer. "I told you to shut the fuck up."

He lashed out so quickly, she didn't even see his arm until it was too late. His fist connected with her jaw and she crashed to the ground.

"Where's the kid?"

Ashton!

Zoe forced herself not to look toward the hall where Ashton was only a few rooms away. *Had he heard the noise? Had he run? Where was he?*

So many thoughts flashed through her head, but the only thing she could focus on was Ashton. Whatever else happened, she couldn't let this man know he was in the house.

"He's not here." She didn't even recognize her voice.

"Where is—"

"I came to get candy," she lied easily. "He's trick-or-treating with his grandma."

The man's lips twisted up and he assessed her for the first time. His beady eyes looked her up and down. "You look like a bit of a treat yourself."

She swallowed hard. Her jaw ached with the action.

The man stepped forward again and instinctively she flinched. But he didn't move toward her, his attention drawn to the fridge this time. And a photo pinned there with a magnet.

While his attention was diverted, Zoe risked a glance to the hall and saw a flash of motion. Ashton peeked around the corner, his eyes wide.

No!

He couldn't be here. He had to go.

Run! She tried to convey the message to him with her eyes. She couldn't risk anything more than that. *Call your dad. Go!*

By some sort of miracle, he seemed to understand her, and a moment later, he was gone.

"What's this?" Zoe turned her attention back to the man as he plucked the photo from the fridge. A second later, he'd bent down, grabbed her by the arm and lifted her up.

He was so fast! He had to be a cat.

He held the picture next to her and grinned. He was missing a tooth and his breath was sour, turning her stomach, but Zoe forced herself to look him straight in the eye. She wanted to remember everything about him.

"Didn't know Wilder had a *mate*." He said the word as if it were something dirty instead of the beautiful thing it was. He sniffed the air and pinched her face between two meaty fingers. "You'll do. The bond between a dumb fuckin' bear shifter and his mate is even stronger than his cub."

The last thing Zoe thought before the man raised his fist and brought it down again against her face was, "No. It's not."

Chapter Eighteen

"SHE'S NOT ANSWERING HER PHONE." Gabe tossed his phone back to the counter. "Where *is* she?"

In the few minutes since Captain Williams had called to tell him that not only had Billy Benson not been recaptured, but had recently been spotted two towns over, Gabe's instincts had taken over.

Zoe. Ashton.

He knew they were in danger. He could feel it. And she wasn't answering her phone.

"Is there a chance she's just not answering your call?" Kade spoke cautiously, and held up his hands in defense as Gabe spun on him. But his friend was right. She hadn't answered any of his calls all week; she was probably just avoiding him. She was probably out trick-or-treating with Ashton the way they'd planned.

But he knew she wasn't. He could feel it.

"I'm going over there." Gabe started to gather his things. He'd radio dispatch on the way over and have someone else take over the Halloween watch group. This was too important. "Maryann said she picked up Ashton fifteen minutes ago. They should be at the house. Where *is* she?" He slammed his fist down and coffee splashed out on the counter.

"Okay," Kade said. "I'll go with you." He turned to Brian, but the wolf was already by his side.

"I'm coming, too. I hope you're wrong, Wilder, and there's nothing to worry about. But if you're not…"

He didn't bother to finish the thought because they all knew what he hadn't said. If Gabe wasn't wrong, and Billy Benson had Zoe and Ashton, he was going to need backup.

Gabe nodded. A second later, his phone rang in his hand. It was a number he didn't recognize but he didn't hesitate.

"Wilder."

"Dad?" Ashton's voice was thin and small and…Gabe's heart stopped at the sound.

"Ashton? What's wrong?"

His voice shook, but Gabe could tell he was working hard not to fall apart.

He was only a kid.

"Dad. He took her. He took Zoe."

"Who?" He didn't need to ask. "Where are you? Are you okay?"

"I'm next door at Mrs. Caldwell's. I used her phone to call you. Zoe told me to go. She *told* me to run. She didn't even say anything, but I heard her." Gabe didn't have a chance to register what that meant, because Ashton was still talking. "I shouldn't have left her, Dad. I'm—"

"You did the right thing. Stay there. I'm sending Brian Blackwood over there to get you, okay? He's going to take you to the ridge until I get back." Gabe didn't even have to ask Brian; with a nod of his head, the wolf shifter was gone out the door and Gabe had no doubts that his son was in good hands.

"Did you see the car he was driving?"

"He took Zoe's truck," Ashton said.

"Zoe's truck? She doesn't—"

"Luke's truck," Kade said next to him, providing some clarification. "She borrowed it."

While Gabe continued to talk to his son, both calming him down and getting as many details from him as he could, next to him Kade was on the phone with Grizzly Ridge.

"Is Zoe going to be okay, Dad?"

"Of course." He hoped he wasn't lying to his son, because Gabe knew without any doubt that if anything happened to Zoe, it wouldn't only be Gabe's heart that would be destroyed —it would be Ashton's too. And he would never let that happen.

He hung up the phone when Ashton told him that Brian was there and, with his son safe, focused his attention on his mate.

"We know where they are," Kade announced. "Turns out Luke left his phone in the truck and he tracked it. It looks like he's taken Zoe to an old hunting cabin. It's off Settler's Road. The guys are going to meet us there. Do you need to call it in?"

He probably should have. Hell, if it were anyone else, he might have. But this was personal, and it wasn't anyone else. It was Zoe.

"I'll call it in," he said after a moment. "Later. But this is a shifter matter. Let's handle it like shifters."

WHEN ZOE CAME TO, the aching in her head had intensified and now was accompanied by sharp pains from her ribs that only just healed up from the last injury.

That asshole had kicked her, too! Rage swelled up inside her and her bear growled for release.

"Easy, tiger." The voice came out of the shadows. "Or should I say, easy, Teddy." The grimy cat shifter came to stand in front of her. "You don't look like much of a cuddly bear, though, do you?" He kicked her again, his foot making contact with her already broken rib, and Zoe cried out.

"Go ahead and scream." The man laughed. "No one can hear you out here. At least not until I want them to."

She needed to shift into her bear. At least then it might be a fair fight. But he had her hands tied in front of her. It wasn't impossible, but it was definitely harder and it would hurt, but—

"Don't even think about it."

She lifted her head and met his eyes.

"I know what you're thinking," he said. "And if you shift into your bear, you're going to find yourself face-to-face with a mountain lion with nothing to lose."

Mountain lion. She knew it.

"What are you going to do with me?" She needed to keep him talking. Because at least if he was talking, she could think about her next step. Maybe she could catch him off guard. He might be a mountain lion with nothing to lose, but he underestimated her. She'd already lost everything. The only thing she cared about now was keeping Gabe and Ashton safe. And there was only one way to do that.

"Oh, I'm going to call your *mate* so he can come and save you, just the way he tried to save mine. And then when he gets here, I'm going to let him watch while I kill you and then I'll kill him. And then, just for fun, I'll go get the kid."

Ashton. No. Icy fear trailed down her spine and her stomach churned. She would not be sick. She had to focus.

He took a step toward her and in a flash, hoisted her to her feet. "But first, we're going to have some fun."

She closed her eyes in the face of his foul breath and tried to turn away but with his free hand, he twisted her head so she was once again looking at him as he backed her up against the wall.

As a bear shifter, she was strong. But he was a cat. His

reflexes were insanely fast. Plus he had at least a hundred pounds on her and with her hands tied in front of her, Zoe was at a huge disadvantage. It was clear what his intentions were.

Panic flash through her, and she had to force herself to focus. She couldn't allow herself to get lost to fear.

Think of Ashton.

"Don't do this." She tried to push against him, but he had her pinned against the rough wooden wall with his hips. She could feel his hard arousal pressed up against her stomach and had to force the nausea down.

Her senses were clouded with his scent, overpowering her instincts. She tried to fight against him as he reached down and unzipped his jeans, but she could only move a little from side to side.

Desperation started to creep in. But no, there was no way she would give up and give in to this creep.

Just when the man moved to pull down the pants of the ridiculous costume she was still wearing, something happened. The hairs on the back of her neck stood up and something inside her leapt to attention.

Gabe.

No. Was it possible? How did he know? Was he—

Before she could finish her thought, the door to the old cabin slammed open. A massive, very angry grizzly bear filled the doorway.

HE WAS GOING to kill him. He was going to rip him limb from limb until he begged for mercy.

Gabe didn't even need the GPS tracking that Kade provided. He would have found her without it.

Zoe's scent. Her fear. Her pain. They filled him.

Gabe and Kade had made it to the edge of town before

shifting into their bears to run through the forest. They could travel faster in their animal form, and he wasn't about to waste one more second. They moved fast, uncaring about the branches that tore at their fur as they crashed through the trees. When the old hunting cabin came into sight, Gabe could sense the presence of the other Jackson brothers.

His brothers. Not by blood. But something almost stronger. Friendship.

Overpowering it all, though, was Zoe. She was scared. She was hurt and she was in trouble.

She was the strongest woman he knew, but Gabe also knew Billy Benson. He was a massive mountain lion. One of the biggest he'd encountered. Also one of the most troubled. He had no family. No connection. And he'd turned to alcohol. A terrible mistake for a shifter with no tether. He was formidable, and worse: he had nothing to lose.

But Gabe had everything to lose. And she was inside that cabin.

Gabe, wait.

Kade tried to stop him, but there was no slowing him down. He didn't slow his pace as he crashed directly into the door of the cabin. He knew without looking that the Jacksons would be right behind him, but Billy was all his.

Zoe's eyes found his immediately.

She was safe.

But that *cat* was on her. *Oh, hell no.*

In a flash, with his cat-like reflexes, Billy spun around, one hand still on Zoe.

Gabe growled.

"Wilder. Nice of you to join us."

He was done with niceties. Gabe stood on his hind legs and roared. The sound shook the walls of the old cabin. Anyone else would have stepped back. But not Billy. He grinned.

"Do you want to watch me kill her?" he taunted Gabe. "Or

maybe I should just kill you so I can have a little fun with your *mate*?" He sneered. "Yes." He nodded. "I think that's the way to go." He moved like lightning and shifted so quickly into his animal that Gabe hardly had a chance to brace himself before Billy crashed into him, teeth and claws bared.

The sting of his claws ripping through his shoulder burned, but Gabe didn't have time to think about it. He bared his own teeth, and lunged forward.

Behind him, he vaguely recognized that the Jackson brothers were there. He also knew they wouldn't step in unless they had to. This was Gabe's fight and they'd let him have it.

Billy's teeth sank into his back leg, and Gabe howled before shaking him free. He twisted and attacked from the side. His claws made a satisfied swipe against Billy's face, but a moment later the cat was on top of him.

His black eyes stared into Gabe's, and he knew he was in trouble because there was nothing but loss reflected back in his blank stare. He didn't have to hear the words to know what Billy was thinking.

This is all I have left.

Billy let out a sound that was part shriek and part howl, and bared his teeth, ready to sink them deep into Gabe's neck. But before the cat could complete his cry, a flash of black fur crashed into him and knocked Billy off him.

Zoe.

She had him pinned to the floor, the roles completely reversed.

He was much larger than her and should have easily been able to overpower her. Especially because she was injured. Gabe could feel her pain. He could also feel her rage. And he knew Billy was done.

So did the Jackson brothers. They all entered the small cabin, filling the space as they waited and watched to see what Zoe would do.

She raised one heavy paw, ready to slash Billy's throat, but she hesitated, and Gabe knew. He couldn't let her do it.

No. He communicated with her.

I have to.

No. He repeated himself.

She looked over at him and for a moment, their eyes locked. *For Ashton.*

Her words, unspoken, reverberated loudly in Gabe's head as she once again raised her paw and brought it down sharply.

Chapter Nineteen

"I'M NEVER LETTING YOU GO."

"You better not."

Zoe nuzzled into Gabe's chest and let the warmth envelop her into a cocoon of safety. After the Jackson brothers pulled her off Billy Benson, the man who she'd learned later was the man who'd defined Gabe's earlier career and almost cost him —and her—everything, and hauled him away, Gabe had wrapped her up in his arms and hadn't let her go.

She was quite content to never let him.

Now that she was back in his embrace, Zoe couldn't imagine being anywhere else. It seemed like a million years ago that she'd tried to convince herself that she belonged elsewhere.

She didn't.

She knew that now.

The only place Zoe belonged was with Gabe.

And Ashton.

It had taken her way too long to sort that out in her brain. And maybe it had taken a near-death experience, or every single thing she'd ever cared about on the line, but now that she had it figured out, she was never going to let him go.

Not for anything.

"You feel so good," he whispered in her ear.

They were lying on the old bed of the hunting cabin where Billy Benson had taken her to hold her hostage. Gabe had wanted to whisk her away and take her back to his house, to town, but Zoe couldn't move. She couldn't leave. And it wasn't just because she wasn't fully healed. Her ribs were still working hard to heal completely.

She had a little bit more healing to do. The important healing. The healing that involved Gabe. And she didn't want to waste even one more second.

"I feel broken." Zoe laughed. "But with you here, I'll be okay."

"I hate that you're hurt."

"I know."

They laid together in silence.

So much had happened to tear them apart. And at the same time, so much had pushed them together. How was she supposed to know what was right?

Listen to your heart.

Her bear, ever vocal, piped up.

But her bear was right. It was long past time that Zoe listened to her and to her heart.

She twisted so she lay on her back. "Can I borrow your cell phone?"

He nodded and reached around him. They'd found some old blankets that were clean and relatively dust free and had laid them down on the old bed. A fire now roared in the hearth and the old hunting cabin had been completely transformed from the prison she'd been captured in only a few hours ago. New memories. That's what was important.

A moment later, Gabe handed her his phone. "You need to make some calls?"

"Only one." She grinned at him, as she quickly scrolled through his contacts and connected the call.

"Hello?"

Her heart was instantly soothed at the familiar voice.

"Hey, buddy." She forced herself not to cry. "How are you doing?" Gabe had already filled her in on Brian Blackwood going to collect Ashton and taking him up to Grizzly Ridge to spend the night, but she needed to hear his voice for herself.

"Zoe? Are you okay?"

She smiled and nodded even though he couldn't see. Behind her, Gabe pulled her close and pressed his lips to her shoulders. "I'm doing okay, buddy. I just wanted to call and let you know how proud I am of you. That was a pretty scary thing, wasn't it?"

"I was brave, Zoe."

"You were." She swallowed back the tears. "You were a very brave little pirate. And I'm so glad you understood what I was trying to tell you. You did the right thing by running away and calling your dad."

"I *heard* you, Zoe."

"You *heard* me?" Behind her, Gabe sat up, obviously listening to the conversation. "But I didn't say anything out loud."

"I know. Cool, right?"

She laughed. "Very cool."

Fated son.

He'd heard her telepathically because they were fated. She'd heard stories about fated mates communicating, but...

Zoe pressed her hand to her chest and finished the conversation. "You have fun at the ridge tonight, okay? The Jacksons will take good care of you. I love you, Ashton."

"I love you, Zoe." The words rolled from his mouth easily. "I'll see you tomorrow?"

"Absolutely."

She disconnected the phone and for the first time in months, everything felt absolutely right. But she still had one more conversation to have. Zoe rolled over, the movement causing her to wince.

"Zoe? Are you—"

"I'm going to be okay." Zoe looked up into Gabe's eyes. "But only if I have you."

She didn't bother sugarcoating her words. The time for playing coy was long since over.

"Gabe, I love you." She looked directly into his eyes while she spoke. "I *need* you."

He moved his mouth to speak, but she pressed a finger to her lips. "Let me finish." He nodded and she continued. "I stand behind what I said before," she continued. "You deserve to have everything you've ever wanted. But I need you to know something." She squeezed her eyes shut for a moment. "You and Ashton, you're all I ever wanted."

Her heart swelled and at the same time broke as she spoke because everything had become so clear for her in the last twelve hours. Hell, maybe it had become clear earlier, but she'd been too stubborn to realize it.

She loved Gabe. He was hers. She was his. Forever. She knew that now.

But, more than that, was Ashton.

Chloe was right. That boy was fated to be her son. And she, his mother.

There was no doubt in her heart that she would gladly give her life if it meant keeping him safe. Maybe she'd needed the dramatic events of the evening to teach her that, but she didn't think so. Zoe felt it deep in her soul. And she always had.

Ashton was her son. Of that, there was no doubt and it was time Gabe knew it too.

SHE WAS SO INTENSELY BEAUTIFUL. Her hair was spread out on the blanket beneath her. Her chest rose and fell in deep breaths, but hitched ever so slightly because of the pain he knew she still felt in her ribs.

If he could take all the pain away from her, he would. Oh, how he wished he could.

"I know that sounds crazy," Zoe protested before he had a chance to say anything. "But—"

He pressed a finger to her lips to silence her. Gabe was done listening to her objections or her reasons she thought she couldn't be with him.

"Stop." His voice was soft, but stern. "I need you to listen to me, Zoe Karrington."

He lifted himself so she was beneath him, safe and protected by his arms. He knew this was one woman who didn't need his protection, but dammed if he wouldn't give his life for her anyway. He knew without a doubt in his heart that he would gladly give not only his whole life, but everything he had, for this woman.

She looked up at him, her long eyelashes blinking mildly as she waited for him to speak.

"Zoe," he said again. "You walked away from me once because you let yourself think something that just wasn't true." She opened her mouth to object again, but once more he pressed his finger to her lips. "You asked me if I could ever love you the way I'd loved Ashton's mother. And the answer is no." She squirmed beneath him, the way he'd expected her to. "But that's because what I feel for you is so much more," Gabe continued. "Marie will always hold a special place in my heart. She was the mother of my son. But you…" He took a deep breath and shook his head as he exhaled. "You," he repeated, "are my fated mate." Gabe paused a beat while those words sank in. "You speak directly to my heart with every breath you breathe." He pressed a hand lightly to her chest. "You are mine, Zoe. And I am yours. And that is something that will never change. No matter how you try to talk yourself out of it. Or, try to talk *me* out of it. Your heart is mine. And mine is yours." He lifted his hand from her chest to trace the mark he'd left on her neck. "Forever."

Forever.

The word reverberated between them.

He'd spoken his truth. He just hoped it was enough. He hoped she understood now. It wasn't about who came before, or the children they had or wouldn't have. It was about them. And if they had each other and if they were strong enough, it *would be* enough.

"Ashton." Her voice was barely a whisper, but Gabe heard his son's name on her lips.

"Yes," he started. "He's—"

"He's mine."

"He's—what?"

Her smile was small at first, but it grew to take over her face. "He's mine," she said again. "He's my son. He's my fated son."

She didn't look away while she spoke so he knew he hadn't misheard. It took a moment for her words to connect with his heart, but when they did, Gabe couldn't stop the smile that took over because it bloomed directly from his heart.

"What do you…I don't…"

"Ashton might not be mine by blood," she continued. "But he's mine by heart. He was fated to be my son."

Fated.

The moment she said the words, he knew them to be true. Zoe was fated to be Ashton's mother.

Zoe worked to push up to a sitting position. "It's the craziest thing," she said. "Or maybe it's not." She laughed and the sound was like the most beautiful song he'd ever heard. "I know you told me that I would never understand what it was like," she continued, and the words coming from her mouth that he recognized as his own cut him like a knife. "It's okay," Zoe said quickly, as if she could see the pain it caused him. "Because I know you thought that was true. And so did I."

Gabe looked at her with fresh eyes, but still, he didn't say anything, waiting instead for her to finish. "I let myself believe that I couldn't understand the love of a mother unless they were *mine*," she continued. "But I know now that I don't need to give birth to Ashton to know he's *mine.*" She sat up and grabbed his hands. "I know this all sounds crazy. But Gabe, I love you. And I love Ashton. You are mine. *He* is mine. Some-things are stronger than blood." She released his hands and grabbed his face instead. "Do you believe that?"

He should have seen it earlier—their bond, their connec-tion. The way Ashton just *knew*. It never should have taken him so long to see what was right in front of his face, but now everything was so clear and he could hardly believe he'd been so blind.

He looked directly into her eyes and, without hesitation, nodded. "Without even the slightest doubt." And then, because there was nothing else to say, he pressed his lips to hers and kissed his mate thoroughly until there was no doubt that not only did she belong to him and he belong to her, but they belonged together. All of them. As a family.

Chapter Twenty

ONE WEEK LATER...

"ARE you sure we can stay here?" It was at least the third time
Zoe had asked Harper the same question, and of course, the
answer was the same.

"Yes." Harper fixed her with a stare across the bed in one
of the guest rooms that they were making up together. "You're
not going anywhere." She wore baby Lily in a sling affixed to
the front of her, and Zoe let her gaze rest on the baby for a few
minutes before turning her attention back to the bed. It no
longer hurt her to see babies the way it used to.

It had only been a few days since Zoe and Gabe had
moved from Gabe's little bungalow in town to stay in one of
the new cabins that had just been built on the ridge. Harper
and Axel, and pretty much all of the Jacksons, had already told
her how happy they were that Gabe had brought her and
Ashton to stay. But still, she worried and the last thing she
wanted was to overstay her welcome, which was why—even

though Gabe insisted she was supposed to be on vacation and taking it easy—she was trying to help out as much as possible.

"After what you've been through," Harper continued. "You should be here. And Ashton…he needs this right now. This…"

"Family," Zoe finished for her.

Because that's what the Jacksons were: a big family. And she was part of that now because, as she'd learned, family wasn't only defined by blood. It was heart. And her whole heart was there with Gabe, Ashton, and the Jacksons.

"Yes." Harper smiled. "Exactly. And you know that you're welcome here as long as you want to stay, now and always."

Zoe nodded. Being at the ridge with everyone was nice, but it was only a little vacation. A chance for them to decompress and recharge after what they'd gone through with Billy Benson. As soon as they were ready, Zoe was looking forward to going home again so they could start their life together as a little family, properly this time.

They finished up with the guest rooms and went downstairs, where Gabe and Ashton were waiting.

"What did I say about resting?" He greeted her with a kiss and pulled her into a tight hug.

"I told her." Harper laughed. "But she won't listen to me."

"That makes two of us." Gabe kissed her again and Harper disappeared to the kitchen, leaving them alone.

"I'm rested," she told him. "I've been sleeping better than I have in weeks."

"Were you guys waiting for me?"

Zoe twisted around to look at Ashton.

"Well, I was thinking of spending some time all together as a family, but our son here has other ideas."

Our son.

The words came so naturally out of Gabe's mouth, because she knew that was how his heart felt. Ashton was *theirs*. And there was no doubt, not to anyone, that she loved him with the same ferocity as a mama bear who'd birthed her cub. *He was hers.* She let the warmth of her love for them both fill her.

"I just want to go with Axel and Ryker," Ashton said. "They're going to that hunting cabin to do some repairs."

It turned out that the old hunting cabin where Zoe had been taken by Billy Benson was on the Jackson property.

It already seemed like a lifetime ago that everything had happened. She'd never felt such rage rush through her before the way it had that night, but she didn't regret her decision. If she closed her eyes, she could still see the look in the cat's eyes as she'd stared down into them. For as big as he was, as strong, and as fearless as he pretended to be, he'd never come up against a mama bear before. And in that moment, it was clear to Zoe that Billy knew he'd been beat.

She could have ended him. But instead of slicing his throat, an action she'd never be able to take back, she'd let her heavy paw land against his jaw, hard. The blow had knocked him out and moments later, the Jackson brothers hauled the mangy mountain lion off to teach him a lesson or two before returning him to the authorities, who'd assured them all that he wouldn't see the light of day for a long time.

In the days that followed, Axel had approached Zoe about the cabin. Did she want them to destroy it? Were there too many bad memories there?

But no. It was quite the opposite, really. Despite the way it happened, that old cabin had been where everything had finally clicked. When she'd finally come into her own as Ashton's mama bear. No, she didn't want them to destroy it.

A plan had been put into place and they'd made the decision to make some repairs and fix it up. With the population on the ridge exploding all the time, they could use the extra space and it could be a unique offering for guests.

"Zoe?"

She blinked away her thoughts and remembered where she was.

"What do you think? Should we let him go?"

"They said I could be their tool boy," Ashton added.

"Tool boy?"

He nodded. "I get to carry the tool boxes and hand them things."

She couldn't help but laugh at his excitement. "I don't see any harm in that," she said as she looked to Gabe, who shrugged. "We'll have plenty of time to do things as a family." *A lifetime.* "Besides," she winked, "I was thinking about how nice it would be to cuddle up in front of the fire in that cabin of ours this afternoon."

"Boring."

They both laughed as Ashton rolled his eyes dramatically.

"Have fun, kiddo." Gabe ruffled his hair.

"And take a coat," Zoe added. "I heard something about snow today."

"And listen to Axel and Ryker."

"I will. I will!" Ashton didn't wait around for more instructions, but spun on his heel and took off out the front door.

"He's happy," she said as they watched him run off.

"More importantly, he's safe." Gabe wrapped her up again and kissed her.

Zoe couldn't get enough of his closeness. She couldn't believe that she'd ever tried to push it away. Even harder to believe that she ever thought she *could.*

"Now how about we go for that cuddle?"

Zoe couldn't think of anything she would like more. But before they could make their retreat to the cabin that was tucked back in the trees, there was a crash in the kitchen. "What the hell?"

They rushed into the kitchen to find Kira, heavy with pregnancy, on the floor. Harper kneeled next to her, a cell phone in her hand.

"What happened?"

"Something's wrong." Kira gritted her teeth and Zoe could see her struggling to take a breath. "It hurts. It shouldn't hurt."

Zoe dropped to her knees while at the same time looking back at Gabe. "Get Nash," she ordered. "Now." Gabe took off without another word, and Zoe turned her attention to Kira.

"It's too soon," Harper whispered.

Zoe looked up into her friend's eyes and saw the worry there. The babies weren't due until January. It was too soon.

"Everything is going to be okay." She smoothed back Kira's dark hair off her face. "Just breathe. The babies are going to be okay. You're going to be okay."

But even as she said the words, Zoe wasn't sure she believed them. Shifter pregnancies could be hard. Very hard. And Kira was pregnant with cross-breed babies. Nobody knew what kind of complications could come from that.

Kira's eyes were wide with fear and whether she believed it or not, Zoe kept on repeating the words. "You're going to be fine. Everything will be okay."

All any of them could do was hope she was right.

I hope you enjoyed Zoe and Gabe's story! There's lots more love to be had at Grizzly Ridge, and still a few sexy shifters that deserve to find their mate. Check out Natalia's story in His to Seek.

For more love and happily ever afters, I have an exclusive sweet novella that's not for sale anywhere. You can read it HERE!

About the Author

Elena Aitken is a USA Today Bestselling Author of more than forty romance and women's fiction novels. The mother of 'grown up' twins, Elena now lives with her very own mountain man in the heart of the very mountains she writes about. She can often be found with her toes in the lake and a glass of wine in her hand, dreaming up her next book and working on her own happily ever after.

To learn more about Elena:
www.elenaaitken.com
elena@elenaaitken.com